DACHSHUND
THROUGH THE SNOW

This Large Print Book carries the
Seal of Approval of N.A.V.H.

DACHSHUND
THROUGH THE SNOW

DAVID ROSENFELT

THORNDIKE PRESS
A part of Gale, a Cengage Company

Farmington Hills, Mich • San Francisco • New York • Waterville, Maine
Meriden, Conn • Mason, Ohio • Chicago

Copyright © 2019 by Tara Productions, Inc.
An Andy Carpenter Mystery.
Thorndike Press, a part of Gale, a Cengage Company.

Thorndike Press® Large Print Core.
The text of this Large Print edition is unabridged.
Other aspects of the book may vary from the original edition.
Set in 16 pt. Plantin.

LIBRARY OF CONGRESS CIP DATA ON FILE.
CATALOGUING IN PUBLICATION FOR THIS BOOK
IS AVAILABLE FROM THE LIBRARY OF CONGRESS

ISBN-13: 978-1-4328-7045-4 (hardcover alk. paper)

Published in 2019 by arrangement with Macmillan Publishing Group, LLC/St Martin's Publishing Group

Printed in Mexico
Print Number: 02   Print Year: 2019

DACHSHUND
THROUGH THE SNOW

It has been almost fourteen years since Kristen McNeil's body was discovered.

Her mother had called the police to say that Kristen had not come home one night, an uncharacteristic action for the eighteen-year-old. But not until thirty-six hours after that was Kristen found near Hinchliffe Stadium in Paterson, New Jersey.

Hinchliffe Stadium was a decayed relic of a time gone by in Paterson. In its day it was the scene of minor league baseball games, high school football, auto racing, and some important boxing matches. But it had fallen into terrible disrepair and wasn't designated as a historical landmark until eight years after Kristen had breathed her last.

So it wasn't exactly a high-traffic area back then, and had some kids not been playing there, it might have been much longer before her whereabouts became known.

The police immediately considered it an

attempted sexual assault leading to the murder, since the victim's clothes were partially torn. The obvious theory was that she had fought hard to protect herself and scratched her killer, since traces of skin were under her fingernails.

The cause of death was strangulation, and in addition to the killer's leaving behind his DNA in the skin under Kristen's nails, the same DNA was found on a piece of discarded gum and a half-consumed beer can near the body. In the intervening years no match had ever been made. The partial fingerprint on the beer can was not enough to yield a match.

Apparently the killer had had no other run-ins with the law, before or since, because his DNA was not in any database. Every few years the Paterson Police ran it through the system, hoping for a match, but they were always disappointed.

The case was famous in Paterson, and occasionally the media would write stories revisiting it. It frustrated everyone that even though absolutely incontrovertible evidence existed to tie the killer to the crime, he was still out there, free.

Also, he might be dead, since it seemed unlikely that someone capable of such a cold-blooded murder would have kept his nose clean for the past fourteen years.

So all the authorities could do was wait for a break that seemed increasingly likely never to come.

Laurie Collins is great on the "giveth" . . . not so much on the "taketh away."

Every marriage should have a balance; I think I read that somewhere once. It works that way with me and Laurie Collins, as she represents the human-decency side of our marriage. It's not that I have inhuman decency, or human indecency; it's just that I am comparatively agnostic on the subject. Fortunately, Laurie has me covered.

Laurie's decency and spirit of giving last year-round, but especially come out during Christmastime. Of course, that would depend on whether your definition of Christmastime coincides with hers. I doubt that it does. I'd be willing to bet that it doesn't.

For years she had viewed Christmas as starting with the conclusion of the Thanksgiving meal. It was a bit early, but on some level it seemed to make sense. Out with the old holiday, in with the new. And here in the Northeast, which is where our home in Paterson, New Jersey, is, the climate has a Christmassy chill in the air by then. For the past two years we've even had white Thanks-givings.

In her eyes, the end of Christmas has always been February 1, though she has never adequately explained the reason for that monthlong extension. I think it is just that she likes Christmas, so why not con-tinue it? It wasn't like anyone was going to stop her; I have long ago ceded control over the family calendar.

Last February, when she retired her Christmas albums for the year and I could finally stop listening to "Jingle Bells," I made the mistake of mentioning that I was pleased that baseball season was about to get going, that "pitchers and catchers" had already reported for spring training. It got her to thinking that if baseball season could last seven months, it wasn't fair that Christ-mas season lasted less than half as long.

"It's only supposed to last three weeks," I made the mistake of pointing out, and in retaliation she decreed that this year Christ-mas in our house was going to be even longer. She didn't invite dissent on the mat-ter.

So our son, Ricky, no sooner took off his

Halloween costume last week . . . he went dressed as an aging Eli Manning . . . than Laurie announced the start of Christmas. Which means the start of giving.

Laurie has never come across a charity she doesn't like. That's fine with me because we are quite wealthy as a result of my inheritance and some lucrative cases I have handled as a criminal defense attorney. She keeps searching for new ways to share our good fortune, and she keeps finding them.

Last year she added a couple of excellent wrinkles to her charitable repertoire. She goes into the local department store in downtown Paterson and writes them a check that they are to apply to layaway items being purchased by their customers.

Her view is that if people are buying gifts on layaway, they must be on the borderline of being able to afford them. So this way when they come in to make their last payments, the cashier tells them that the gifts have already been paid for and hands them their items. It's like a Christmas present for those struggling to buy Christmas presents.

Her other new trick is even more personal. The local post office, as well as a couple of retail stores in town, puts a tree in their lobby. Children then fill out a small form asking for special gifts, and those are put in envelopes and hung on the tree. Laurie takes a bunch of them and anonymously makes the wishes come true.

No place would think to install a Christmas tree the first week in November, so Laurie has approached the places and requested the wish lists of children who have already submitted them, in anticipation of the tree being set up. The stores know that Laurie is dedicated and totally reliable, so they are happy to give the wishes to her, and she is happy to fulfill them.

So that's what she is doing today, as a way to celebrate the start of her extended Christmas season. She's opening wish cards from our local pet store, occasionally laughing and more often crying. Some of them can be pretty poignant and heartbreaking, such as when children ask for a pair of shoes, or a warm coat.

Laurie has a rule: if she opens a wish card, she will make it happen, no matter what. I cringe at the possibility that some kid is going to request a Porsche, or a mail-order bride.

The kids include their address so that the donors will know where to send the gifts. Laurie goes to the stores and personally picks out everything. She then carefully wraps the gifts, sometimes including a card from Santa, and then sends them by UPS.

She generally does not include me in doing this, which I'm absolutely fine with. Occasionally she'll mention a wish that seems funny, or maybe particularly sad, but basically it's her thing. So right now she is doing her thing and I am fulfilling my own wish, which is to sit on the couch and watch ESPN.

"Andy, listen to this. It's from a boy named Danny Traynor." She starts reading the note, which starts with the traditional "Dear Santa." " 'Santa, I know I always ask for stuff, but this time it's important. Can you please give us a coat for my mom and a sweater for my dog Murphy? He's a dachshund, so it has to be a long one. And then I have a special request for my present. Please, Santa, please find my dad and bring him home. Thank you. Your friend, Danny.' "

"Uh-oh."

"We need to get into this, Andy."

"Get into it how? The kid's father might have run off with his secretary, for all we know."

"Maybe, and if it's something like that, we can back off. But we're investigators; let's find out."

"You're an investigator; I'm a lawyer. If

the kid wants to sue his father, that's where I come in." Laurie was a lieutenant in the Paterson Police Department and has served as my chief case investigator ever since she left that job.

She nods. "Fair enough; I'll look into it myself. I have another job for you anyway. This one is right up your alley. It calls for a lawyer and dog lover, and you check both of those boxes."

"I do not like the sound of this." Laurie knows that I have been trying to get out of the lawyering business for a long time now. Unfortunately, I keep getting roped into taking on cases.

"Actually, I think this one is perfect for you. You might even have some fun."

"You know I don't like fun. I have never found fun to be any fun. I'm funny that way."

She nods. "I'll tell you what. Let's go interview your potential client, and if you don't want to take on his case, then no problem."

No way am I going to get out of meeting this person, and in truth I'm as intrigued as I'm going to get. I don't intrigue easily. "Now?" I point to the television. "While they're talking about the Giants?"

Instead of answering, she picks up her

15

phone and dials. Someone must answer because she says, "Does now work for you?"

I assume the answer is yes since Laurie hangs up the phone, stands, and says, "Your client meeting is about to begin."

"Where are we going?"

"Eastside Park."

"Can we take Tara and Sebastian?" Tara is my golden retriever; she is widely and correctly recognized as the supreme living creature on all planets so far discovered. Sebastian is our basset hound. He doesn't aspire to such heights; basically all he wants to do is eat and sleep.

"Absolutely," Laurie says. "They will fit right in."

I know every inch of Eastside Park.

Not only did I grow up playing Little League and high school baseball on its fields, and tennis on its four courts, but it is where as a teen I hung out with friends trying to pick up girls.

It would be accurate to say that I had better success at baseball and tennis.

Now, since the park is only about seven blocks from my house, it's where I take Tara and Sebastian when I want to give them a long walk. That happens almost every night, so by this point there is likely not a blade of grass that one of them hasn't pissed on.

We enter as always through the Park Avenue entrance. It's a Thursday afternoon so few people are here; they're all at work.

Suckers.

A police car is parked near the tennis courts, and we walk in that direction. Stands are always set up for spectators, maybe enough to hold forty people. That's more than sufficient; it's not like they play the US Open in Eastside Park.

As we get closer, I see that a uniformed police officer is sitting in the first row of the stands, and with him is his partner, a beautiful German shepherd. I turn back toward the police car, and sure enough, on the side is writing identifying it as a K-9 unit. Nobody is playing tennis for them to watch, so it's a pretty good bet that this is who we are here to meet.

"You want to fill me in on what's going on?" I ask Laurie.

"Corey can do that."

I look toward the court, trying to get a better look at the waiting cop. "Is that Corey Douglas?"

"It is."

"He and I have an unpleasant history."

"Time to turn the page, Andy. What's past is past. Don't look back. Time to forgive and forget. Let bygones be bygones."

"What are you, a cliché machine? I am not representing that guy. He's nuts."

About three years ago I cross-examined Sergeant Corey Douglas about his actions on a case. I don't remember all the details, but the cross did not go well for him. I nailed him for not having probable cause to

18

take the actions he took, and all the evidence he accumulated was ruled inadmissible.

It wasn't highly unusual, until he came at me in the parking lot afterward. He was furious with me, which in itself doesn't make him at all unique among police officers I encounter. What struck me is that his anger was on behalf of his dog.

The dog, whose name I believe is Simon, had performed great work in the operation, at some risk to his physical well-being. Douglas was outraged that Simon's success, and the risks he had taken, now were rendered worthless by the court.

He saw it as my fault. Which, I suppose, it was.

Douglas didn't attack me physically in the parking lot, which was rather lucky for me, since he has me by forty pounds and four inches. He's also not a coward, which gives him another advantage over me. But for a few minutes I thought he was going to lose it, so I got out of there as fast as I could, and I haven't seen him again until now.

We reach them and Laurie says, "Corey, Andy . . . I believe you already know each other?"

He and I both nod, and I throw in a small sneer for effect. Never let it be said that Andy Carpenter is mature. Tara and Sebastian, meanwhile, are not holding a grudge against Simon. They are sniffing away at each other.

Laurie smiles. "Good; this is a special moment. Corey, why don't you explain the situation to Andy?"

Instead of doing so, he says, "How about if we talk about the fee? If it's too high —"

Laurie interrupts, "There is no fee, Corey. If Andy does this, it's out of the goodness of his heart."

Are you out of your mind? is what I want to scream at Laurie. But when it passes through my wimp filter, it comes out as "I have a lot of heart goodness; I'm known for it."

Corey seems unappeased; maybe he thinks that I should pay him to be his lawyer. Finally he says, "We can table that for now. I'm retiring next month; I've put in my twenty-five."

"Good luck with that," I say, staring my version of a dagger at Laurie. "I keep retiring, but it never seems to take."

"Simon — his full name is actually Simon Garfunkel — just turned nine." Corey points to him. "We've been together seven years; I want him to retire with me. But retirement age for police dogs is ten."

I know that the policy among police forces

nationally in recent years is to let a dog live out his retirement years with his handler, should the handler want him. "So will they be giving Simon another handler for the next year?"

Corey nods. "Yes. Dogs now are trained to specialize, whether it be in apprehensions, locating suspects, drug interdiction, whatever. Back when Simon was trained, they taught them to do it all. They're planning to move Simon to the drug detail when I leave."

"What's the problem?" I ask.

"His hips are acting up, and those drug-detection dogs are on their feet all day. It won't be good for him. Plus, he's put in enough time and service; they should let him live out his years with me. He deserves that. He loves me, and I love him even more."

I see Laurie fight off a smile; she knows that's the kind of pitch that will get to me.

"Have you taken this up the ladder?"

He nods. "I talked to the captain and got nowhere. Then I took it to the Appeals Board and they blew me off. That's when Laurie suggested you."

"So you want me to represent you in court?"

He shakes his head. "Not me. Simon."

This time Laurie is unable to fight off the smile. "Simon would be your client, Andy."

"Can I talk to him privately?" I ask.

"Sure," Laurie says, and she leads Corey out of the stands, walking off toward his car. Simon, Tara, Sebastian, and I are left alone.

"Simon, you've had enough of this working crap?"

He licks my arm as I scratch his neck, so I take that as a yes.

"And, Tara, you're good with this?"

I swear, she smiles at the prospect, so that's another yes. I don't bother asking Sebastian since it would involve waking him.

"All right, let's go for it." I get up and walk them all back to where Corey and Laurie are waiting.

"What was that about?" Corey asks.

"I can't tell you what we talked out because of lawyer-client confidentiality." Laurie rolls her eyes. "But I have decided to very temporarily come out of retirement to represent Simon. Okay?"

Laurie leans over and gives me a kiss on the cheek. I take that as a yes.

Corey's reaction is slightly less heartwarming. "You know, I almost killed you in the parking lot that day."

"It's just as well that you didn't."

"Paperwork would have been ridiculous," he says. "Plus, I like Laurie."

"That's why I keep her around."

This one is not going to be easy.

I'm meeting at our house with Hike Lynch, the lawyer who works with me when I take on a case. Hike is a terrific researcher and has quickly gathered a great deal of information both on animal law in general, and police policy toward animals in particular.

Hike is by nature a total pessimist, not just in his work, but in his life. He is positive that everything will turn out badly, and when it doesn't, he views it as proof that the next thing will turn out twice as bad. Hike considers the future, whether ten seconds or ten years away, to be something to fear.

But my concern about this case is not based on Hike's description of it as a "total, wall-to-wall loser." Considering his normal point of view, that could actually be described as almost upbeat. Unfortunately, I don't see much here to work on; no law limits police discretion in handling their working dogs.

There are laws against animal abuse, but in no way does this go anywhere near that standard. Simon is not being tortured or confined or starved; the police are simply insisting that he continue the job for which he has been trained, in accordance with long-standing department policy.

While we're talking, I get a call from Dr. Dan Dowling, Tara's and Sebastian's veterinarian, which in my mind makes him the "vet to the stars." I had asked Corey Douglas to take Simon in for a full medical examination, and Dowling is calling to give his report.

"I did a full workup, Andy. X-rays, blood work, all of it."

"What did you find?"

"For a dog his age he's in good shape. Only abnormal test result was his thyroid level, and even that's not too far off. It's easily handled with Soloxine, which I gave Sergeant Douglas."

"What about his hips?"

"That's definitely an issue. He's got some arthritis. It's not overly dramatic for a shepherd his age and history, but it's there and it's concerning."

"Is he in pain?"

"Definitely would be feeling some discomfort," Dowling says. "Shepherds are stoic, so it's not obvious, but it has to be there."

"If for the next year he is on his feet all day, every day, will that worsen the condition? Can he even do it?"

"I'm sure he can manage to do it, but it will take its toll on him later on, and it will certainly increase his discomfort."

I get off the phone and share the news with Hike, who of course says it works against us. "Arthritis is nothing; everybody's got arthritis."

"I didn't realize arthritis was nothing. Thanks for sharing that."

"Are you kidding? I've got arthritis that has arthritis."

The idea of Simon's possibly being in pain and moving with difficulty in his retirement annoys the hell out of me. "They're treating him like a dog."

"He is a dog," Hike points out.

"He's an employee; he's a cop. He has spent his life protecting your arthritis-ridden body. If he was human, they would be reacting differently; they'd give him a gold watch, and an early retirement with a pension."

"What are you saying? That they're discriminating against him because he's a dog?"

"Exactly."

"Andy, even though you don't, the world treats dogs differently than humans. And it works both ways; sometimes the dog is better off. For example, dogs can piss and shit on the street. If I tried to take a dump on the street, I'd be arrested, and it wouldn't matter how many plastic bags I brought to clean it up."

"You'd have to represent yourself in court; I'm not going anywhere near that."

"You know what I mean."

"And what I mean is that they are discriminating against a longtime employee because he happens to be a dog. If we don't stop this, it will be a slippery slope. Cats, fish, monkeys . . . you name it, they will become second-class citizens."

"Do you hear what you're saying?" Hike asks. "They're not citizens at all; they're dogs, and cats, and fish, and monkeys."

"Simon is an employee, pure and simple, and the establishment is stepping on him because of who he is."

"So where exactly are you going with this?"

"We are about to sue the city of Paterson for species discrimination."

When Laurie gets home, I can tell she's upset.

Hike is still here, so I won't find out what's going on until he leaves. Laurie is not about to open up in front of Hike; she knows with complete certainty that whatever the problem is, he'll make her feel worse.

I don't think that I've done anything to upset Laurie; our relationship is surprisingly drama-free. But it's always possible, and I'll be relieved when and if I find out that I'm an innocent bystander in whatever is going on. I see myself as an observer of the human condition, not a cause of it.

Hike and I are pretty much done anyway; we have our legal strategy in place. I send him on his way with two assignments. One is to prepare the papers for a lawsuit we are going to file against the City of Paterson, and the other is to talk to Sam Willis.

Sam is my accountant and resident computer genius. He's capable of finding anything that can be accessed through the internet, legally and otherwise. The good news is that every single thing in the world can be accessed through the internet.

Sam's research will be crucial in our case preparation, and Hike will give him the particulars as to what we need. I also know that Sam will get right on it; he loves investigating almost as much as he dislikes accounting. Besides, Sam is a dog lover.

Before Hike leaves, he counsels me not to get my hopes up. "This is going nowhere. Simon is going to die on the job."

"Keep thinking the good thoughts," I say.

Once Hike leaves, I don't have to prompt Laurie to tell me what's on her mind. "I spoke to Mrs. Traynor."

"Ricky's teacher?" I regret the words as soon as they leave my mouth; I'm somehow not able to remember our son Ricky's third-grade teacher's name in the moment, but I know that Traynor is not on the list of possibles.

"No, Andy. Ricky's teacher is Ms. Zimmerman."

"Right. I knew that; I was testing you. Good old Zim; they don't make them like that anymore."

"She's thirty," Laurie says. "Julie Traynor

29

is Danny Traynor's mother. He's the little boy who left the wish on the tree."

I nod. "Got it."

"So I called her, told her that I had the gifts that Danny asked for. She knew what I was talking about, but she said Danny wrote it himself. I asked if I could bring them over, and she hesitated, but finally said it was okay.

"They live on Thirtieth Street just off Broadway; the upstairs apartment in a two-family house. Obviously not very well off financially, which explains the wishes. By the way, the dachshund is adorable."

"What about the missing father?"

"I'm getting there. She was grateful that I brought the stuff, especially since Danny was at school. She said that they've had to tighten their belts lately, but didn't say why. She's going to hold on to it and give it to him at Christmas."

"They haven't started Christmas yet? Don't they realize that Halloween is over?"

"Andy . . . She seemed wary, like she was worried about talking to me. I wasn't going to bring up Danny's missing father, but it was part of the wish, so . . ."

"You had no choice. The god of wishes says it is so, and it must be so."

"Don't make fun of me, Andy. I told her

that Danny asked if we would find his father, and it was like I shocked her with electricity. She told me that her husband was fine, and he wasn't missing, and that Danny had a wild imagination."

"You didn't believe her?"

"She didn't have to be hooked up to a poly for me to know that she was lying. I told her that I was an investigator and a former cop, and that you were an attorney. She had heard of you. But she was more afraid of me than anything."

"Maybe she just considers the subject personal. And it is personal; maybe their marriage is splitting up, or he's having an affair, or she's having an affair, or who knows what. It's not our business, Laurie."

"Maybe. But I was getting a weird vibe, Andy. This woman was scared, of her situation, of me, of the world. I think there is something going on there. I offered to help in any way I could, but she wanted none of it. She made that very obvious."

"She could be scared that her husband ran off and left her to take care of their child by herself."

"Maybe." Laurie's tone is the opposite of *maybe*.

Her instincts in matters like this are excellent, but that is sort of not the point.

"Maybe there is something going on. But no matter what is wrong, it doesn't involve us, no matter what the kid wished," I say.

"I want to help her, and I really want to help that little boy."

We hear a noise outside.

Laurie glances quickly at her watch. "Ricky."

It's the school bus, and Laurie and I both go outside to meet it. Laurie picks Ricky up and gives him a huge hug. She looks like she is going to crush him. Ricky looks at me as if to ask, *What the hell is going on?*

"Ricky, just go with the flow. It's Christmas."

Noah Traynor watched the end of his life through the window of his motel room.

It was not unexpected; far from it. On some level he found it relieving; it had been a while since he had had any kind of control over events, and this was sort of making it official.

For the better part of ten days he had lived in this Paramus motel, not far off Route 4, leaving only to get his meals. His entire focus during that time had been on finding a solution to his predicament.

He had come up with absolutely nothing, and now it absolutely did not matter.

He could see the motel parking lot from his room, and farther in the distance the street behind it. That's where they parked, so as not to call attention to themselves. The two cars were unmarked, but the four men that got out of them couldn't have been police officers more obviously if they had had their ranks tattooed on their foreheads.

Traynor knew that there must be others, probably uniformed, parked outside his line of vision. Coming in force like this was understandable, but ultimately unnecessary. He was not going to resist.

He watched the plainclothes officers coming toward the motel until they split up into pairs and went to each side. They would be taking the stairs to the second floor, where Traynor's room was.

He wasn't at all surprised that they had found him; truly disappearing in this age of technology and information would take much more expertise and effort than Traynor had summoned. It didn't matter how they did it, but he figured they probably traced his calls to Julie and then used the GPS built into his phone.

Whatever. They were here.

Traynor wanted to avoid the drama and violence of their breaking into the room, so instead he went outside and waited for them just beyond the door. He raised his arms in the air so there would be no confusion or misunderstanding.

Eight men appeared, the four in plainclothes and four in uniform. They drew their guns when they saw him and approached.

"Noah Traynor?"

"Yes."

They ordered him to put his hands against the wall and frisked him to make sure he wasn't armed. Then they read him his rights.

"What are you charging me with?" he asked, though he knew.

"The murder of Kristen McNeil."

"I'm innocent," he said, knowing that they were probably the most meaningless words he had ever spoken.

"Everybody is, Traynor," said the arresting officer. "Everybody is."

"I need your help, Vince."

Vince Sanders is the editor of the local newspaper and one of the two people whom I share a regular table with at the wondrous establishment known as Charlie's Sports Bar. I knew Vince would be here tonight; if he wasn't, it would mean he was dead, which would have seriously impacted his usefulness to me.

Our other tablemate is Pete Stanton, captain in charge of Homicide in the Paterson Police. Pete is also here to eat and drink and watch sports, in this case NBA basketball. Vince and Pete watch sports because they are die-hard fans; they eat and drink because I pay all the checks.

Life for Vince and Pete is simple.

"You want my help?" Vince says. "I'm sort of busy now, so I don't really like the sound of that."

"Really? Tell me if you like the sound of

this." I call to the woman who has the misfortune to be our every-night waitress, "Sheila, from now on Vince is going to be running his own tab."

Vince sits up as if I'd put a hot poker up his ass. "That Andy is some kidder, huh, Sheila? Disregard anything this funny guy says." Then he turns to me. "I am a friend, and friends are here to help. Tell me what I can do."

"This is nauseating," Pete says.

I speak to Vince. "I want you to run a human interest story about a dog."

"There's a surprise," says Pete, who has never understood my love for dogs.

"Don't listen to him," Vince says. "If it's a human interest story, then humans are interested in it, and humans buy newspapers. If I run it, it might help circulation. So it's good for business and helps my wonderful friend Andy. It's a win-win." Then, "And you'll keep picking up the tab in here, right?"

"The birth of a Pulitzer," Pete says.

"So what's the story?" Vince asks.

"I don't want to tell you in front of Sergeant Schultz over here." I point to Pete. Since the story involves a lawsuit that we are filing in the morning against the Police Department, I don't want to give Pete a heads-up. "I'll come to your office in the morning to tell you the story and bring photos."

Vince nods. "Will you by any chance be bringing doughnuts?"

"I'll stop and pick up a dozen."

"Chocolate-cream filled?"

"Is there any other kind?"

"I look forward to seeing you," Vince says. "Have I mentioned how much I cherish our friendship?"

While Vince is pouring on the bullshit, Pete has taken out his phone and is looking at it. "Good news. You can talk away, geniuses. I've got to run."

"Off to arrest another innocent person?" I ask.

"Dream on, counselor." Then Pete looks at his half-eaten plate of burger and fries. "Looks like you didn't get your money's worth tonight."

Once he leaves, I tell Vince the story about Simon and describe what I want Vince to do. He actually takes notes, and when I'm finished, he asks, "Are you still coming to my office in the morning?"

I shake my head. "No, not necessary anymore. I'll email you the photos."

"What about the chocolate-cream-filled doughnuts? I believe you mentioned something about a dozen."

"Not happening."

"This is very disappointing."

When I get home, Laurie sees me pull up and comes out on the porch to greet me. This is rarely a good sign, especially since she's not smiling.

"Did you hear what happened?" she asks.

"I doubt it."

"They made an arrest in the Kristen Mc-Neil murder."

"Good. That must be why Pete left Charlie's when he did." My reaction did not take into account that Laurie does not seem happy. Usually an arrest of a murder suspect would be considered good news, so there must be more to it. "Is there a problem connected to this?"

"The person they arrested is Noah Traynor."

The name sounds familiar, but I can't place it. I do know it's not Ricky's teacher. "Refresh my memory."

"He's the father of Danny Traynor, the boy who asked us to find his father."

"Poor kid; I feel for him. But his father appears to have been found."

"Technically speaking, he asked us to bring his father home. That has not been accomplished."

"Uh-oh."

We head into the house; I follow Laurie into the den, where she has two glasses of wine waiting for us. This is a disaster waiting to happen; nobody pours glasses of wine in advance of what is meant to be a casual conversation. And the rest of the bottle is on the table as well; this could go on for a while.

I usually play the role of counterpuncher in situations like this, and it rarely works out. It's time to be aggressive. "Laurie, the kid wrote a note, put it on a tree, and you did your best to make it come true. This is not a blood oath."

"I took the note; that comes with a responsibility."

"Play this out. You think if you didn't take it, then Sherlock Holmes or Perry Mason would have come along and grabbed it? And they would have proven the father innocent? Your winding up with the note did not ruin the kid's chances of getting his father back. And if you're feeling guilty, put the note back on the tree. Then it's somebody else's problem."

"I know you don't understand."

"What do you think the chances are that he's guilty?" As an ex-cop, Laurie always instinctively feels that the police would not make an arrest without a strong probability of guilt. As a defense attorney, my natural view is opposite of that.

She thinks for a moment. "Without knowing the facts? Ninety-five percent."

"And if he did it, if he murdered that young woman, you think he should go home to his wife and kid and dachshund?"

"No. Of course not."

"Good."

She nods. "Then we agree. If we look into it and don't think he's innocent, we back off. You're the best, Andy."

How the hell did that happen?

Vince must love his free food and beer.

The story in the paper is absolutely perfect. A photo of Corey Douglas's spectacular German shepherd accompanies it on page one, and it reads like the Paterson Police Department is trashing an American hero.

Which in my view they are.

Hike has filed a lawsuit on Simon's behalf seeking expedited relief, warning that a delay would result in immediate and irreversible harm to our client. Dr. Dowling has sent a letter, which we included in the filing, basically supporting that position.

I went one step further and enlisted the help of Rita Gordon, the chief clerk at the courthouse. Rita is a good friend and was also a participant in a forty-five-minute affair with none other than yours truly, Andy Carpenter. It took place after Laurie went back to her hometown of Findlay, Wisconsin, to take the job of chief of police.

The affair lasted the full forty-five minutes for the same reason some prizefights go the distance. The obviously superior fighter will carry the lesser opponent so as to give the viewing audience their money's worth and a good show. In our case Rita was clearly the titleholder, and while I wasn't technically the viewing audience, she generously gave me an outstanding show.

Since then we've maintained a close friendship punctuated by sexual banter, and Rita can often be helpful as I try to navigate the court system. She is also a dog lover, with two mastiffs of her own, so she was the ideal candidate for the task at hand.

Rita has manipulated the system to make sure that our filed petition lands on the desk of Judge Seymour Markinson. Judge Markinson, though he shares his colleagues' disdain for me and my courtroom antics, absolutely loves dogs. If anyone would be willing to see past the irritation that I represent to protect Simon, he's the one.

Corey has taken a risk by allowing himself to be quoted for Vince's article, which might provoke some retaliation by his bosses in the Paterson PD. He's even doing a couple of follow-up interviews with other news outlets who are picking up the story.

Even though he's retiring, his bosses can

still cause him aggravation, so it's all pretty gutsy on his part. But to me it's a clear sign that he cares about Simon.

I've taken a chance by going so public with this, especially so early. It will certainly generate the grassroots support that I want; no one living on the New Jersey section of Planet Earth would back the Paterson PD over a hero dog.

But it could definitely get the opposition's back up. They might resist simply to show that they cannot be intimidated, and definitely not by an annoying defense attorney.

My being an annoying defense attorney, though, is why I took this approach. Corey had already gone about it the right way. He had spoken to his superiors, and when they'd refused his request, he had followed proper procedure and gone to the Appeals Board. He got nowhere; they brushed him aside.

The chance that Andy Carpenter would go through the same "proper" channels and get a different result is pretty close to absolute zero. It would also be considerably less fun and much less satisfying. If these jerks can't find it in their hearts to let Simon retire a year early, after all he has put in, then they deserve to be publicly humiliated.

Which is where I come in.

Hike and I are in my office going over the information that Sam Willis has dug up, as well as deciding who we will call as witnesses. That's all dependent on Judge Markinson's granting the hearing that we've requested. If he doesn't, then we've gotten dressed up for a party that doesn't exist.

As we're wrapping up, Rita Gordon calls me on my cell. "The judge is pissed."

"How pissed?"

"He mentioned something about disemboweling you with a butter knife."

"Did he smile when he said it?"

"Andy, you didn't need to turn this into a public relations thing. You know that judges do not like to be pressured."

"I wasn't pressuring him; I was pressuring the Paterson PD."

"That's what I told him," Rita says.

"What did he say to that?"

"That's when he mentioned the disemboweling."

"Did we get the hearing?" I ask, since that is all that matters.

"Friday at ten A.M."

"Rita, you are fantastic."

"I am keenly aware of that."

So things are looking up. We've got the hearing we've been seeking and are pretty well along in our preparation. The other

45

good news is that while Laurie has been looking into the arrest of Noah Traynor, she doesn't seem to have found anything that would call for us to intervene. It's possible that she is relaxing her self-imposed rules on being a Christmas-wish genie.

I head home to take Tara and Sebastian for a walk and wait for Ricky to get home from school. Tonight there is both NBA and college basketball to watch on television.

Life is good.

The first sign of life's possibly not being as good as I thought is a strange car in the driveway of our house. This isn't necessarily a problem, but I have a sense of foreboding.

When I get into the house, Laurie hears me and calls out, "Andy, we're in the kitchen." My keen sense of deduction tells me that "we're" refers to Laurie and the driver of that car.

When I get to the kitchen, I see that Laurie is having coffee with a woman I don't recognize.

"Andy Carpenter," Laurie says, "meet Julie Traynor."

I have a feeling life just took a turn for the worse.

"What's going on?" I ask, after the requisite hellos.

"Julie called and asked if she could come over, and she's just arrived," Laurie says. "So we can hear what she has to say together."

Tara and Sebastian are lying at Laurie's feet, munching on chewies. Their expressions are impassive; they are obviously as much in the dark as Laurie and me.

"I'm sorry I was so cold to you when you came over," Julie says to Laurie. Julie's voice and demeanor scream out *distraught*. I've had rectal exams that I've looked forward to more than this conversation.

Julie continues, "But I was already so worried and frightened, and when I heard that you had been a police officer, I guess I was afraid to trust you."

"I understand," Laurie says, which makes one of us.

"But then when Noah was arrested . . . you know about that?"

Laurie nods. "We do."

"I didn't know where to turn," Julie says, then turns to me, meaning that she may have figured out where to turn. "My cousin is a lawyer; his name is Marvin Simmons. He's not a criminal attorney . . . he works for an insurance company. But when he heard that I had sort of a connection to you, he said that your reputation is that you're the best."

I don't know her cousin Marvin, but I already hope he and his company never win another case.

"Andy is definitely the best," Laurie says, obviously casting her lot with Cousin Marvin.

"We don't have much money," Julie says, "but I would pay whatever you charge no matter how long it takes me."

This is not getting better as we go along. "Why don't you tell us your story," I say. "That way we will have a better sense of where things stand."

"There is simply no way that Noah killed that girl. If you knew Noah, you would know that it is simply an impossibility."

"Why do the police think he did?"

"DNA. He had a brief relationship with

48

her and was with her outside that stadium, just before it happened. He knew he must have left DNA that the police would have gotten. It was about two years before we met. He was just a kid. But they could never connect him to it because they didn't have his DNA on file.

"Then Noah's brother, who didn't know anything about this, sent his own DNA in to one of those websites . . . you know, those genealogy sites? They tell you your nationality, connect you with relatives . . . things like that. Once Noah heard about that, he knew this day was coming."

I know what she's talking about. People get their DNA results, then upload them to a website that tells them about possible relatives they have, but might not know. Uploading the information removes the right to privacy, and the police can access those databases. Once they saw Noah's brother's DNA results and matched it up against the evidence from the murder, it was an easy next step to go after Noah.

"And you knew about his connection to the murdered woman all these years?"

"He told me about five years ago. I wanted him to go to the police, but he said that they would arrest him. It's not like he could direct them to the real killer. So we've lived in fear."

"What more can you tell us?" Laurie asks.

"I don't know all the details. But if you would talk to Noah. Please, if you would just talk to him."

"Of course we'll talk to him," Laurie says.

If I say, *No, we won't,* I don't think it will go over well. And the truth is that I feel sorry enough for Julie Traynor to at least want to do that much for her. It doesn't mean I think her husband is worthy of representing; a wife thinking her husband is innocent is not exactly an earthshaking development.

So I throw in an "Of course," accompanied by a nod. It's the closest I can come to a ringing endorsement.

Ricky walks in, having just been dropped off by the school bus. Laurie introduces him to Mrs. Traynor, and his presence will effectively end the talk about murder. Too bad he didn't get here sooner.

Tara and Sebastian both go over to Ricky to get their expected petting, and he is only too happy to oblige.

"My son, Danny, is about your age," Julie says. "He loves dogs too."

"Do you have one?" Ricky asks.

She smiles and nods. "We do. His name is Murphy and he's a dachshund."

"What do they look like?" Ricky asks.

She shows all of us a picture of Murphy that she has on her phone. He's adorable, which I admit grudgingly, because if not for Murphy, Danny would not have placed a wish on the pet store Christmas tree. And I wouldn't be going to the jail to talk to an accused murderer.

"Wow," Ricky says. "What a cool-looking dog. Can I come see him sometime?"

"Sure," Julie says.

Once Julie leaves, we all go for a family walk in Eastside Park. This time we don't run into any cops with their police dogs; it's just a pleasant, slow, incredibly comfortable walk, during which Ricky tells us about his day at school. For the moment I am not even thinking about Julie or Noah Traynor.

Life is once again good . . . it does seem to bounce up and down a lot.

Laurie comes with me to the jail to talk to Noah Traynor.

I register as his attorney, listing Laurie as my associate. That enables us to meet in a private room, outside the range of prison microphones. At least that's the way it is supposed to be; one never knows.

Noah is brought into the room in handcuffs, as is customary, and the guard attaches those cuffs to the metal table. Then the guard takes a position outside the only door to the windowless room. It's a good bet Noah is not going to be able to use this meeting as an opportunity to escape.

He's about six feet tall, thin at maybe 160 pounds. Like all incarcerated people, especially first-timers, he looks scared. But that's not the dominant aspect of his appearance. Trumping it all is that he looks tired.

"I've been running in place for fourteen years," he says, after we introduce ourselves.

Then, "Thank you for coming here. I'm very glad that Julie has not lost her power of persuasion."

"Just to be clear," I say, "we are here to listen and gather information. We have not committed to represent you, nor have you asked us to."

He nods. "I understand. The public defender has been here and handled the arraignment. I pled not guilty."

I nod. "I know. Why don't you just tell us your story from the beginning."

He nods. "With all that has gone on, over so many years, there actually isn't that much to tell. I was nineteen years old when I met Kristen McNeil in a bar. It was called the Moonraker and was on Route Four in Paramus. It's not there anymore."

"How long did you know her before her death?"

"About three weeks. But I only actually saw her three or four times. She was very secretive about it; she didn't want me to meet her friends or even spend time with me in public."

"Did she say why?"

"No. I asked her but she sort of shrugged it off. I figured it must have had to do with some other relationship she had; as it turns out, she had an existing boyfriend, but I didn't know that then. The truth is that I found her attractive, so I was fine with it."

"Did you have sex with her the day she died?" Laurie asks.

"No. I wanted to, and she said she wanted to. That was the reason we went out to that part of town."

"So describe what happened that day," I say.

"We met near the Falls, near Hinchliffe Stadium. It was pretty much understood we were going to have sex; we had danced around the idea, but we both knew. I brought some beer, and we were drinking. Not too much; certainly neither of us was drunk.

"She had been acting strange . . . I told you that . . . but I thought that just might be who she was, you know, high-strung and unpredictable. But then she started telling me that I had to take her with me when I left."

"Left for where?"

"College. I was leaving a few days later to go to the University of Maryland."

"Why did she want to go with you?"

"I don't know, but she said she couldn't live here anymore, that she had to leave. I asked why she couldn't just leave on her own, and she said she had no money. It was like she wanted to go with me and then live with me in secret. Really bizarre."

"What happened next?" I ask.

"When I didn't say she could come with me, she started to lose it, like she was panicking. I held her arms, trying to calm her down, and she scratched my face. I was bleeding. The whole thing was crazy and sure as hell wasn't what I expected when I went there."

"Were her clothes already torn when you left?" Laurie asks, since they were torn when she was found.

"No. Not by me, and not that I saw."

"What did you do then?" I ask. "After she scratched your face . . ."

"I left. I mean, the whole thing had blown up."

"Did she leave also?" Laurie asks.

"No. She was sitting there crying when I left. She had her own car, so I didn't think I had to worry about her. And the truth was, I wanted to get as far away from her as I could. Things had not exactly gone according to plan, and the truth is I was scared of her and what she might do."

"What happened next?"

"I didn't think anything happened, at least at first. It wasn't until a couple of days later that I even heard about it. It was all over the news. They were calling it an attempted sexual-assault murder. Since she had scratched me like that, I thought they would think I killed her."

"So what did you do?" I ask.

"Nothing. Absolutely nothing. Unless you consider panicking and freaking out to be doing something. I thought they'd come for me, but they never did. Gradually I began to believe that they had no way to connect the two of us. Over time I read up on things and realized that I wasn't in any DNA data bank. And since none of her friends knew me, I wasn't on the police radar."

"And you never told anyone?" I ask.

"I may have mentioned her by name to one or two people; I honestly can't remember. But I certainly never talked about it after she was killed; the first person I finally told was Julie."

It wouldn't have mattered either way whether he told someone that he knew her; with his DNA on the scene, there would be no way to claim otherwise. And his claiming innocence after the fact wouldn't matter either, as it would obviously be viewed by the prosecution as self-serving. "Didn't you want to help find the real killer?" I ask.

He nods again. "Yes, of course, but I had nothing to offer. And then, as time went by, it would look worse and worse that I waited so long. So I did absolutely nothing; it was like I was frozen in place. I'm not proud of it, but I didn't see any other option at the time."

"And you saw nothing unusual as you were leaving?" I ask. "No people, no cars that seemed out of place? That's a desolate area."

"Nothing. Why would I want to kill her? It doesn't make any sense. I'm not a violent guy; I've never even been in a fight. But what if I was? What would I have had to gain from killing her?"

He goes on to talk about the DNA test his brother took, and how he realized that would eventually become his undoing. It's the same story that Julie told us.

"No one will believe me now," he says, probably accurately assessing his situation. "Not after all these years."

I tell him that Laurie and I will talk about this and get back to him. "In the meantime," I say, "I assume the public defender has instructed you not to talk about these matters to anyone."

"He has."

"It's excellent advice; follow it."

"So, do you believe him?" I ask, once we're in the car.

Laurie thinks about it for a few moments. I'm not sure what to expect. As an ex-cop she is always late to the party when it comes to believing protestations of innocence. But as a granter of Christmas wishes, she wants little Danny's to come true.

"I'm torn," she says. "We're not talking to the person who might have done this. That person was nineteen years old; this is a full-fledged adult. He could have done something bad then, maybe even accidental. Assessing him now is very difficult; we would have had to know him back then to have any chance of knowing the truth."

"Yet assess we must."

"We don't even know the circumstances. If it were a cold-blooded premeditated killing, I might be more likely to believe that he didn't do it. He was a kid attracted to a girl that was going to have sex with him; why would he want to kill her?"

"What about his not reporting it? Consciousness of guilt?"

She nods. "Maybe. Or panic, or a young person making a bad decision."

"So where do you net out on it?"

"I'm torn, and not just because of the Christmas wish thing. I know that has to have its limitations. But if he's innocent, and I admit that is a very big if, I want him to have a chance. And while I know the public defenders are good, hardworking lawyers, they are overloaded. I just don't think they have the time or resources that would be necessary in a case like this."

I'm at a loss here. I thought Laurie would have a strong point of view on this, since strong points of view are a specialty of hers. My role is traditionally to take the other side; if she was in favor of defending him, or against, I could simply take whatever the opposing position was and argue it. I'd lose, but at least I would be comfortable with the ground rules, and we would have talked it out.

But Laurie's being unsure is disorienting and leaves me without a strategy. Worse yet, it puts me in the decision-making role, which doesn't suit me at all. As roles go, I would do better playing Lady Macbeth.

"What do you think?" she asks. It is the question from which there is no defense.

"I'd like to talk to Billy." Laurie knows that Billy is Billy Cameron, nickname Bulldog, who is the head of the Public Defender's office. "He'll tell me the straight story."

"About what?"

"About Traynor's life in the intervening years since the murder. Here's the thing: I have no idea if he's telling the truth or not. But he could be; it's credible that a nineteen-year-old kid would act the way he acted. Not admirable, but credible.

"But if he's lived a life on the straight and narrow ever since, then that would be compelling to me. I think it's rare that these things happen in isolation. If Noah Traynor strangled Kristen McNeil, then I doubt the incident turned him into a Boy Scout."

"So you'll talk to Billy tomorrow?"

I shake my head. "Tonight. Tomorrow I have a German shepherd to defend."

When we get home, I call Billy. I hope he'll tell me that while he's obligated to defend Noah, he's as evil as they come. He doesn't; he says that the limited background information they have gathered already shows the exact opposite.

"He could use you, Andy." While that may be true, Billy is thoroughly biased. He would like nothing better than to dump this off on me and thereby lower the workload on his exhausted staff.

"I'll get back to you," I say.

When I get off the phone, I tell Laurie about the conversation.

"The other thing to keep in mind is what Julie said about paying your fee," she says.

I nod. "Somehow I don't see myself collecting money every month from a poor woman with a son and dachshund."

Laurie smiles. "That is tough to picture."

"Maybe I can make up the difference by charging Simon the German shepherd double my normal fee."

She nods. "I think he'd be fine with it." Then, "Does this mean you're taking the case?"

"He said he's been running for fourteen years. One way or another we need to get him to the finish line."

"I love you, Andy."

"As well you should."

Simon is looking good this morning.

Corey must have taken him to the groomer yesterday in anticipation of his court appearance, because he's looking sharp and spiffy. Unfortunately, and the mistake is mine, I didn't want him looking sharp and spiffy.

We are arguing that he is not physically able to perform his job, so my preference would have been for him to look weak and haggard. But I failed to mention it to Corey, so that is on me.

A big crowd is on hand; the gallery is filled to overflowing. That is no doubt the result of the publicity campaign we engineered, and it could possibly annoy Judge Markinson, who Rita said was already pissed off. Nothing I can do about that now.

Sitting at the defense table beside me are Corey, Hike, and the aforementioned spiffy-looking Simon. He has his own chair and is sitting up on it attentively; I almost expect him to ask for a pen so he can take notes.

At the opposing counsel's table are three people. I only recognize one of them. She is Sara Hopson, a Police Department lawyer and, I am sure, the lead counsel. The other two people are either lawyers or paralegals; I'm not sure which and couldn't care less. Sara will be in charge.

Sara's presence is ironic since I know her to be a dog lover. I know that because she and her husband adopted a Lab mix from our Tara Foundation, the dog rescue organization that my former client Willie Miller and I run. Sara must not be happy to be here today, but it's her job.

Just before Judge Markinson comes in, Corey asks, "What do you think? Do we have a shot at this?"

I shrug. "A puncher's chance." A snorting noise comes from the other end of the table; it could have been Simon but more likely Hike.

Judge Markinson comes in and views the gallery with obvious displeasure before taking his seat at the bench. He sternly states that we are not conducting a "sideshow" and threatens to clear the courtroom if there are disruptions. It seems like a premature threat, but one that shows he is irritated by the publicity.

Which means he is mad at me.

Judge Markinson explains what is about to happen, that this is a hearing to determine whether our lawsuit has the merit to go forward. The Paterson PD has asked for a dismissal of our suit, and however the judge rules will indicate which way he thinks the ultimate verdict will be rendered.

Before we begin, Sara asks that Simon be removed from the courtroom, citing courtroom rules that only service animals are permissible inside. What she really wants is to eliminate the media eating all of this up and taking our side.

"Your Honor," I say, "Simon is the definition of a service animal; he has served this community for his entire life. He is also the petitioner in this action and should therefore be entitled to be present. Lastly, he is not being disruptive and is completely housetrained."

A slight titter from the gallery stops when Judge Markinson gives the room his fierce stare. "I'll allow Simon to remain, though I will revisit the decision if in fact he becomes a distraction."

Since we have brought the action, we are up first. I am going to call only two witnesses favorable to our position, one in the beginning and one at the end. In the middle, I will be calling one person from the opposition camp. I've given our witness list to the court in advance, so in that sense there will be no surprises.

Our first witness is my vet, Dan Dowling. "Have you examined Simon?"

"I have. A few days ago. I did a full workup, including blood work and a set of X-rays."

"Can you describe his physical condition?"

Dowling nods. "In many respects it is quite good for a dog his age and with his life experience. But his hips are a significant issue and concern." Dowling describes a deterioration and arthritis in the hips, a progressive condition, meaning it will become worse over time.

"His bosses are set on transferring him to drug enforcement and detection, which will mean he will be on his feet all day, every day. How will that affect him?" I ask.

"It will hasten the deterioration. I have no doubt he has discomfort now, and that will substantially worsen. It would be the opposite of being in his best interest."

I introduce videos of Simon taken five years ago, running in the park with Corey. Then I show another video of him running last week and ask Dowling to point out the differences in Simon's gait, attributable to the hip issues. It is a dramatic way to show what has happened to him over the years.

"Is it likely that his seven years of service to the department has contributed to the deterioration?"

"I don't think there's any question about that. A German shepherd's hips have just so much wear and tear in them. His lifestyle and profession would have to have caused considerable stress on them."

I ask a few more questions, then turn the vet over to Sara.

"Dr. Dowling, is Simon capable of doing the job to which he is being assigned?"

"I'm quite sure he is, at least right now. German shepherds are stoic."

"Do you have any way to know how the alleged problems with his hips have progressed over time?"

"No, I've only examined him now." Dowling then drops a mini-bomb. "I requested previous X-rays from the department, but was told they do not exist. That was disappointing on several levels."

She ignores that. "Are there medications that could help him?"

"Definitely there are meds that could help with the discomfort, though not with the deterioration. Checking through the records, I was struck by the fact that he has not been given that medication. It should be prescribed immediately." Dowling is killing Sara; I may have to nominate him as Witness of the Year.

"Isn't a common sign of pain in a dog a reluctance to eat?" she asks.

"Often so, yes."

"Does Simon look malnourished to you?"

"No."

"Thank you. No further questions."

The phone had not rung in almost fourteen years.

Actually, it was the phone number that had not received any calls; the physical phone had been replaced six times. But its mission had never changed: it existed only to receive a call from one specific client.

The phone belonged to Charles Arrant, and although it had not rung in almost a decade and a half, Arrant was not in the least bit surprised to see that streak come to an end. He devoured the news religiously, possibly because he was frequently the cause of it, so he knew exactly what to expect.

That is not to say that there hadn't been other kinds of communication between the caller and Arrant. Arrant had been receiving money, substantial money, frequently. And he had been facilitating connections between the caller and many of Arrant's other clients. But everything had been done electronically, protected by encryption, not by personal contact.

Arrant was in the hotel gymnasium on the exercise bike when the call came. Through the glass he could see the outdoor pool, shut down in deference to the onset of cold weather. He couldn't see the indoor pool from that vantage point, but he made good use of it every day.

He lived in hotels, a different one in a different city every month. He had not made a bed, cooked a meal, or paid a heat or water bill in a decade. Other people served him, and he paid well for the privilege.

Arrant was known in his professional world as a specialist. He didn't agree with the characterization because while a specialist by definition focuses on one type of activity, Arrant was the master of many. He had few clients, but whatever they wanted him to do, it could accurately be said that he specialized in doing exactly that.

It should be noted that the name Charles Arrant no longer existed in any meaningful way in his life. He had not used it in more than a decade, ever since the first Red Notice had come out. Instead he used a series of identifications that were prepared by experts, and virtually invulnerable to exposure as the fakes that they were.

He didn't say *Hello* when he answered the phone; he remembered with a small smile that this client considered it a wasted word. "You've been following the developments?" the client asked, starting the conversation as if they talked every day.

"I have."

"Get involved."

"I could use more specific instructions." Arrant thought he knew what the client meant, but it was prudent to be sure.

"Monitor the situation and report back to me."

"Understood."

There was no reason to discuss financial terms; money was never an object. There would not have been an opportunity to discuss them anyway, because as soon as Arrant said, "Understood," the client clicked off.

It was time for Arrant to get off the bike and go to work.

My next witness is Lieutenant Thomas Quinto.

Quinto is in charge of the K-9 unit and is Corey's and Simon's boss.

"Lieutenant, can you please tell me department policy towards early retirement in the case of injury sustained on the job?"

He seems confused. "You mean for dogs?"

"I mean for police officers."

"If you're talking about humans, it's not really my area, but I believe that early retirement is often granted in cases like that. But dogs —"

I interrupt, "Thank you. Does this summarize department policy, to your knowledge?" I offer into evidence a copy of a page taken from the *Paterson Police Administrative Policies and Guidelines,* handing copies to the court clerk, the judge, Sara, and Quinto.

"I believe it does, yes," Quinto says.

"Can you point out to the court where it is mentioned that it only applies to human officers?"

"Well, it just assumes."

"So it doesn't specify that it only pertains to humans?"

"Of course not; there would be no reason to. But they're definitely talking about humans."

"Are you admitting to the court that the department engages in species discrimination?"

"Come on . . ."

"Is that a yes?"

He shakes his head. "No."

"A canine is less of an officer of the law than his human counterpart?"

"Let's just say he's different."

"Lesser?" I ask.

Quinto thinks for a moment, looking for a way out. "In some ways."

"Has Simon performed his job well during his career with the department?"

"Absolutely."

"Heroically?

Quinto shrugs. "I guess, but that's what he has been trained to do. So . . ."

"Ah," I say, as if that clears it up. "It's not a big deal that he is a hero because he's had training. Wait a minute, don't human officers have training as well? Or do they just show up one day and grab a badge?"

"It's a different kind of training."

I nod. "Because they are different skills. But you see dogs as lesser officers with lesser rights?"

"In some ways."

"Do you remember an incident that took place three years ago, involving a bank robbery at First Savings and Loan?"

He nods. "Yes. Simon trapped two of the thieves and it resulted in their capture."

I ask for permission to play a short video clip on the courtroom monitor. It's a press conference, being conducted by Richard Melnicker, the Paterson chief of police.

He is smiling as he answers a question from the assembled press. Standing behind him is Lieutenant Quinto, who is nodding as Melnicker speaks. "And special thanks goes to Simon, without whom this operation would not have been so successful. We value our canines as much as we value any of our officers; they work tirelessly and are heroes, as Simon demonstrated today."

"You were nodding in agreement with what the chief was saying?" I say.

"I knew what he meant."

I nod. "Yes, it was fairly straightforward. Was the chief wrong?"

"No."

"He was telling the truth as he saw it?"

"Yes."

"Lieutenant, why are you taking the position that Simon has to work one more year?"

"It's not my position; it's department policy."

"There's the handbook; can you show me the policy?"

"It's based on long-standing precedent."

"So dogs have previously applied for early retirement before and been denied?"

"No, this is a first."

"Thank you."

Sara tries to rehabilitate him by pointing out differences in the way dogs and human officers are treated and dealt with. Basically, it is a recitation of what Quinto has always assumed to be department policy.

We break for lunch, and I will use the time to get ready to wrap up our case. I feel like it is going well, if only because not a single member of the general public will want to see Simon forced into a job that will be painful and contribute to his deteriorating health.

More important, not a single member of Paterson's elected government will want to see the general public not get what they want.

By the time I get done with them, mobs will be in the street chanting their demand: *FREE SIMON GARFUNKEL!*

"He's the best partner I've ever had, and I've had some great ones."

Corey is on the stand talking about Simon, who sits on his chair staring straight at his friend, though able to avoid blushing at the praise. I had told him not to show emotion, but said it was okay to wag his tail, and he's doing that now.

"Can you talk a bit more about that?" I ask. I generally avoid open-ended questions like that, even to friendly witnesses, but in this case I want to open a lane wide enough for Corey to drive a truck through.

"Sure. He is always there, totally present and in the moment, every day. He never has a bad attitude and never complains about anything. He is fearless; he would go through a brick wall to protect me and to do his job.

"But more importantly, he's my friend. He senses when I'm down, or upset, or scared, and he tries to make me feel better. And he does, every single time.

"I love that dog, and I don't want him to be hurting. He's done so much for me, for this department, for this city, that he deserves to live out his days in style and comfort. He's not a possession of the department; he lives and breathes and hurts and loves unconditionally. And anyone who says otherwise doesn't know what the hell they are talking about."

I don't say anything for a while; I don't ask a question or make a sound. I just let Corey's words settle into the courtroom; I would bet that not a person within the sound of his voice does not feel a clenching in their throat, or moisture in their eyes.

Game, set, and match.

Sara has no questions for Corey and changes her plans to call an officer in the Paterson PD Administration. He was going to talk authoritatively about department policy toward animals, which would now probably get him tarred and feathered by the gallery.

Sara knows when it's time to stop digging.

Judge Markinson gives us the opportunity to make a summation, sort of a closing argument. Because we went first in presenting our case, Sara gets to go first in this stage:

"Your Honor, I'm a lover of dogs; I have two of my own. I am also an admirer of them, and Simon is worthy of that admiration. I have seen canines in action, and I believe they love their job. We need them to do it, and they do it well.

"But we have rules and policies in place, very similar to those in place throughout this country. They are not onerous, and they are not cruel. They balance care and compassion for the dogs with the needs of the community they protect.

"I recognize that this may not be the popular position to take. In a perfect world everyone, human and canine, could retire when they wanted to and live a life of leisure. But the world does not work that way, and it's in many ways good that it doesn't.

"Simon has a job, and a purpose, and he should be allowed to finish his work. Then, God willing, he can spend his remaining years being doted on and fed biscuits. Thank you."

My turn. "I am sure that Ms. Hopson is sincere in what she says. I certainly know for a fact how much she loves dogs. But there is one important way she is wrong.

"She talked about policies that balance the needs of the community with compassion for the dog. But that is a fallacy. Those policies are rigid; that's why we are here today. And there is no planet on which inflexibility and compassion can coexist; they are by definition incompatible.

"I played for you an example of a high-ranking police official praising Simon and saying that he sees no fundamental difference between canine and human officers. I could have shown you ten other examples of the same statement, made by other high-ranking officials.

"But they are talking the talk without walking the walk. Because a human officer in Simon's exact situation would get the compassion that Simon is being denied. He or she would get early retirement, and a pension."

I smile. "As Simon's attorney, I can tell you that he is happy to forgo his pension. But he is not willing to give up his rights.

"I know something about dog rescue, and I know that there are many, many wonderful dogs, currently homeless and with bleak prospects, who could be trained to do this kind of work. There is no reason to work a dog like Simon until he hobbles in pain from deteriorated hips. We owe him much,

much more than that.

"Let the next generation take over, while we honor our elders.

"Simon and Sergeant Douglas and I thank you."

When I sit down, Corey leans over and says, "Great job. I'm glad I didn't kill you in the parking lot."

I expect Judge Markinson to retire to chambers to consider his ruling, and it's even quite possible that he will delay it and announce it on the court website. But he surprises me.

"I will obviously issue a full, written opinion. But I can safely say that this matter will be allowed to proceed, and I think the plaintiffs have a substantial chance of prevailing on the merits. If the parties cannot arrive at an amicable solution, a trial date will be set." He stares directly at Sara when he refers to the possibility of a settlement; his meaning is clear.

He adjourns the hearing and Corey asks me what this all means.

"As much fun as it would be to take this to trial," I say, "I'm pretty sure that Simon is going to be sleeping in a lot."

"If you want me to, I will represent you."

I've come down to the jail to inform Noah Traynor of my decision. I have second thoughts even as I'm saying it, but the die is cast.

"I want you to," he says without hesitation. "Thank you. But I also want to be straight; I can't imagine what your fee is, but right now I am unable to pay it." He looks at his handcuffs. "And I'm not really in a position to earn a lot of money."

"I understand. Let's not worry about that now."

"I will make good on this, as long as it takes." He describes what he does for a living: a freelance writer, he sells articles and essays to magazines, both print and online. Then, "Hopefully I'll be able to write in here."

"Right now we need to forget about my fee and focus on proving your innocence," I say, having absolutely no idea if he is innocent.

He sighs. "Sounds good to me. I'm scared as hell."

"You wouldn't be normal if you weren't. For now I want you to write down everything you remember about that incident. I want to know where you were the other times you saw Kristen, any friends of hers that you might have met or that she mentioned, anything she ever said that in retrospect seems strange to you, everything and anything. Don't worry if it seems important; if you remember it, I want to know about it."

"Okay."

"Anything else you want to tell me now?"

"This is going to sound a little weird, but I kept a scrapbook about the murder."

"A scrapbook?" I don't like the sound of this, and it sounds a bit worse than "weird." Killers commonly keep a scrapbook of the media coverage of their "work"; it can be a source of demented pride and pleasure to them. Juries tend to look at them with more than a little suspicion.

"Well, not a real scrapbook. I mean, I didn't paste them down or anything. But I did follow all the media coverage because I was scared I'd be mentioned. I saved it all in an envelope. There might be some information in there that you can use."

"Where is it?"

"At my house. Julie can give it to you; it's at the top of the bedroom closet."

"Okay, I'll get it."

As I'm leaving, he says, "During this process, if you learn anything important, good or bad, will you tell me?"

"I'll keep you as informed as I can. But these things take time."

He nods. "I know. I just keep thinking about Julie and Danny, especially Danny. Julie is tough, and she understands what's happening. But Danny . . ."

He doesn't finish the sentence; he doesn't have to. I leave and call Laurie to tell her that I'm heading to the Traynor house, and she says that she'll meet me there. She seems unusually protective of Julie Traynor. I'm not sure what Laurie is worried about; it's not like I'm going to say anything mean.

On the way I call Billy Cameron and tell him that I've taken the Traynor case. He doesn't try to talk me out of it; I get the feeling he's tossing confetti while we're still on the phone.

"You need any of our clerical staff to help out, let me know," he says.

"I won't."

"Good. Because I can't spare anyone." He's still laughing as he hangs up.

When I get to Julie Traynor's, Laurie is already there, as is Danny and the dachshund, Murphy. Danny is a cute kid, but humans as a species have a cuteness ceiling that they cannot exceed. Not so with dogs, and especially not with dachshunds. Murphy is at a level beyond adorable.

I join them in a cup of coffee and briefly play a video hockey game with Danny. He destroys me, as Ricky always does. It's a generational thing.

I had told Laurie why I was coming by, so she goes over to Danny and Murphy to keep them occupied while I talk to Julie. "Noah said there is an envelope at the top of his closet. He wants me to have it."

She nods, clearly knowing what I'm talking about. She goes into the bedroom and comes out with a thick manila envelope that must weigh two pounds. "Here it is. I hope it helps."

I nod. "Me too."

"I feel so much better with you on the case."

This time I don't say, *Me too.*

The climb up Legal Mountain always begins with a meeting.

We get the staff together at the beginning of a case to go over the early details, and to prepare everyone. All of the people in the meeting, most especially me, know we've got a daunting task ahead of us that will take huge expenditures of time and effort.

Even though I liken it to mountain climbing, the two have basically no similarity to each other. Legal cases I understand; as much as I might dread them, they make sense and are a necessary evil. They have a purpose and a result, and they serve a societal need. They also have an end result; circumstances are significantly altered no matter how a case ends, at least certainly for the defendant.

Recreational mountain climbing is different; I don't understand it and I don't know why it exists at all. It ranks with skydiving and suicide bombing as the three leisure-time activities I am least likely to pursue.

Friends of mine once ascended to the Mount Everest base camp. That didn't sound so bad or crazy; my initial impression on hearing it was that they probably hung out at the lodge, sipping hot chocolate by the fire. Not only that, but guys called Sherpas carried their stuff for them, sort of like permanently assigned personal bellmen. I figured I could get into that, providing there were enough rest stops and indoor plumbing.

As I found out more, it turns out that wasn't quite their experience. Apparently, mountain climbing consists of starting in a place where there is plenty of air to breathe, and gradually reaching an altitude where, if you can find any air at all, you'd better suck it down before it runs out. Finding random pockets of oxygen is like trying to get a final couple of M&M's out of an already-empty bag.

It's also freezing cold. Yet despite that it gets colder and the air gets thinner the higher you go, mountain climbers inexplicably keep heading in that direction. That gives new meaning to the phrase counterintuitive.

They live on rations that the North Korean army would turn up their noses at, and at every single moment there is a serious danger of falling thousands of feet to a certain death. Continuing to live often depends on one's ability to drive metal stakes into solid, frozen rock.

Then, if an avalanche has not swept the climbers away to a frozen suffocation, they make it to the top. They're so happy to be there that they celebrate the moment by turning around and trying to make it back down to where they started, where the air and food and heat are plentiful. It never seems to dawn on them that they could have just stayed there in the first place.

Nowhere along the entire up-and-down trek is there a flat-screen TV or wireless internet, and good luck trying to find a Sherpa who can tell you how the Giants did that afternoon.

Put in that context, starting a legal case doesn't seem quite that bad, but I still complain about it. And it all begins with the staff meeting.

As always, we hold it in my office on Van Houten Street in Paterson, on the second floor above the fruit stand owned by Sofia Hernandez, who is my landlord. The conference room is small, but since I'm not planning on expanding my staff anytime soon, it will serve our needs for the foreseeable future.

Present, besides Laurie, Hike, and me, are Sam Willis, Willie Miller, and Marcus Clark. Sam, my accountant and office neighbor in real life, is the computer and technical guy for the team, and his value increases with every case. Willie has no assigned role; he is my former client and current partner in the Tara Foundation dog rescue. But he is also incredibly tough and is fearless. These two qualities I do not possess in abundance, or even in minute quantities, so he often comes in handy.

Marcus Clark is a top-notch investigator, but that is not what makes him unique on the planet. He is the toughest person that was ever invented; he could have handled himself and physically dominated at any time and place in history, and I'm including when dinosaurs roamed the earth.

Marcus has functioned many times as my bodyguard and protector, and if not for him, people would long ago have been talking about me in the past tense. But even though he is on my side, he scares the hell out of me.

Last to arrive is my assistant and self-described office manager, Edna. She likes working even less than I do; the difference is that she doesn't actually do any work. My taking on a client is enough to put her into a depressed funk that usually lasts until the jury reaches a verdict.

Edna looks and sees that the entire group has already assembled and says, "Sorry I'm here . . . I mean, sorry I'm late." It would not take Sigmund Freud to see through Edna.

I stand and open the meeting. "Our client is Noah Traynor. You've probably read about him in the newspaper; he has been arrested and charged with the murder of Kristen McNeil, fourteen years ago.

"We're just getting started, so there's not much for me to tell you yet. We have copies of media articles written contemporaneously with the crime, and in the years since. It will at the least give you the bare bones, until we receive the discovery.

"Sam, do what you can to supplement this. I'm sure you can find out plenty online, so just feed it to us when you have it."

While I am talking, Marcus gets up and looks outside the window. I don't know what he's doing and am afraid to ask. Even if I did, he would just grunt an answer that I would find incomprehensible. When I'm trying to have a conversation with him, I always find myself wishing I had a Google translator that I could set to "Marcus to English."

The group has a bunch of questions, few of which I can answer. It's just too early in the process to know much; that will soon change.

Marcus again gets up and looks out the window, but this time he turns and makes a slight head motion to Laurie. She stands and the two of them go into the reception area to talk about something, though I don't have a clue what that is.

Moments later they come back, and Laurie says, "We may have a bit of a situation here."

Nobody, most definitely including me, has the slightest idea what Laurie is talking about.

But the tone in which she has spoken, and that she seems to be channeling something straight from Marcus, is the reason for the dead silence in the room.

Laurie continues, "I don't want anyone to look out the window, but Marcus had noticed when he arrived a man sitting in a gray Toyota 4Runner near the end of the block, across the street from the check-cashing place. He took notice of it because he's Marcus, and because there seemed to be no reason for the guy to be there.

"The guy and the car are still there, and he appears to be focused on this direction. It's possible that he's watching for a delivery of ripe melons to the fruit stand downstairs, or that he's doing one of a hundred other things that have nothing to do with us.

"But Marcus is suspicious, and I think we should accept that as serious. Marcus, have I left anything out?"

"Nunh," Marcus says, adding his typical light conversational wit to what might otherwise be a tense moment. But Marcus does have remarkable instincts in situations like this, so I will be surprised if he's wrong. Surprised but pleased.

"So here's what we are going to do," Laurie says. "Marcus is going to leave here first. If the guy downstairs follows him, then Marcus will successfully deal with him. If not, then Marcus will move into position where he can watch the watcher."

"You want me to come up behind the guy?" Sam says. "I could be on him before he knows it." Sam always wants to get in on the action, but except for me and possibly Edna, he would be the least capable person in the room to handle it.

"No, Sam," says Laurie. "I think we should follow the plan I've just laid out."

"This is not good," says Hike, who wouldn't know "good" if he were bathing in it.

Willie doesn't say anything because he doesn't have to. He knows that we all know he is ready for anything and everything.

Laurie continues with the plan. "Once

Marcus is in place, we'll all leave gradually, either one at a time or in pairs. Just get in your cars and leave when it's your turn; if the guy follows you, then Marcus will be there to handle things. If not, you've got nothing to worry about.

"Andy, you and I will go last. We'll leave together, but since we each have our own car here, we'll obviously split up."

Everybody nods their agreement at the plan. Marcus leaves first, and about ten minutes later Laurie's cell phone rings. Marcus says that the guy did not follow him. Marcus is now in position, so we can start sending people down.

We choose Edna and Hike to go next. Edna is picked because she seems the least likely to be the target of surveillance, so we might as well get her out of the way. Hike is included because we're still here, and it always brightens up a room when Hike leaves it.

In only a few minutes Marcus calls and pronounces Edna and Hike free and clear. Sam Willis goes next, then Willie Miller follows. The subsequent calls come from Marcus: they have not been followed.

But the guy in the Toyota remains in place, apparently watching the office entrance. I know of no reason why Laurie or I would be subject to this kind of scrutiny, and possibly this is a false alarm, but we're about to find out.

Laurie and I go downstairs and out the front door together. Fortunately our cars are in different directions on the street, so we each go our own way once we're outside.

I start to drive home, and within three minutes my phone rings. Laurie says, "It's you."

"The guy is following me?" I ask, despite already knowing the answer.

"Yes."

"What should I do?"

"Just drive home as you normally would; Marcus is watching him. I'll see you at home."

The rest of the drive takes about fifteen minutes, all of which I spend unsuccessfully trying to figure out what this could be about. Situations like this are usually related to cases I handle, but I haven't exactly been a workaholic lately.

The obvious possibilities are the Noah Traynor case or my representation of Simon the police dog. It seems inconceivable that it could be the latter; my opposition was the police department and I don't see any reason they would want to track me. Shoot me, yes. Track me, no.

Of course, my pursuer could be doing more than surveillance; he could be intent on hurting me, or worse. But even the Traynor case doesn't seem to make any kind of sense as a cause of all this; it hasn't really begun. I haven't even read the discovery yet, no less started investigating. Who could I possibly be a threat to?

It's also possible that it's from a previous case that is no longer active. Despite my relentlessly sunny disposition, I have definitely made my share of enemies. I've even been the cause of a number of people going to prison.

I have no way of knowing if the surveillance, if that's what it is, started today. We only know about it now because we were with Marcus. This could have been going on for a while; no way would I have picked up on it. If it had been up to me to discover it, it could have started in the Carter administration.

I get home and park next to Laurie's car in the driveway. I walk to the front door without looking around; I just have to have faith that Marcus is doing his job, and I know he is. But it's still nerve-racking.

When I get inside, Laurie is just getting off the phone. "Ricky is sleeping over at Will Rubenstein's tonight," she says. Because we were going to be in the meeting, Will's mother, Sally, had picked them both up at school and taken them to their house. "Until we get a better idea what's going on, it's best he not be here."

She no sooner says that than the phone rings again. She answers and says little, just a couple of *Right*s and *Okay*s, topping it off with "I agree."

"Marcus?" I ask when she hangs up.

She nods.

"What was it you agreed to?"

"That Marcus is not going to grab the guy now; he's going to watch him and not do anything until we can figure out who he is and what he's trying to do."

As much as I don't like the idea of being followed like this, it seems like a logical plan. "Please mention to Marcus that if the guy is about to shoot me, he should intervene."

She smiles. "If I think of it, I'll tell him."

The discovery documents have arrived, and they don't offer much.

I already know most of the facts of the murder, such as they are, from reading the media coverage that Noah had culled. The discovery provides some extra details, but not many.

The main connection tying Noah to the crime is DNA, proving he was with the victim close to the time of death. The skin under the fingernails also demonstrates that they had a physical altercation, so that is particularly damning evidence. The DNA evidence is all a jury would need, especially in light of Noah's actions, or inactions, after learning of the crime.

The value of these documents to us is that to some degree they give us an investigatory road map. The police conducted many, many interviews, as they are wont to do. They talked to all of Kristen's friends, her boyfriend, and even a few people they considered potential suspects.

But everybody had an alibi, and no one besides Noah left DNA and skin at the scene. That trumped everything.

The documents describe Kyle Wainwright as Kristen's boyfriend at the time of her death. Kyle's relationship with her, and that it had seemed to be ending, initially placed him dead center on the police radar. However, he was quickly eliminated as a suspect as he was on a college visitation trip at Tufts when she was killed.

Another interesting note is that Kristen had been acting a bit strangely in the days before her death, which is consistent with what Noah told us. Friends reported that she seemed nervous and worried and even talked about going somewhere else to live, which is again what Noah described. That could all have been tied into having a secret, "forbidden" relationship, but for now we have no way to know if something more ominous was going on.

Significantly, at no point in the past fourteen years did Noah's name even come up. None of Kristen's friends mentioned him, nor did anyone else that was interviewed. She had clearly kept him a secret. If Noah is telling the truth, and Kristen wanted him to take her away with him, then not revealing his identity to anyone would help conceal where she ran off to.

Starting right away, we will begin interviewing anybody and everybody who might have information helpful to our defense. We'll be coming at those talks from a different point of view than the police did; their focus was that whoever was with Kristen, having not come forward, was the killer. We will be assuming the opposite about Noah.

Of course, they might have been right.

I interrupt my reading to have an early dinner; Laurie has made her special-recipe fried chicken. It is fantastic; if I am ever able to successfully give up lawyering, I've got an idea to buy a million buckets and sell the stuff.

The doorbell rings while we're having coffee and I immediately tense up. I can't imagine Marcus would let some bad guy just walk up to the house, ring the bell, and shoot me, but you never know.

While I'm trying to figure out what to do, pretending to contemplate as I wipe the nonexistent fried-chicken crumbs from the side of my mouth, Laurie goes to the door. She seems not to possess my coward gene, an obvious accident of birth.

I can't see who it is, but I hear her say,

"Corey, come on in." This immediately tells me two things: Corey is here, and he's coming in.

Both Corey and Simon are here, which delights Tara. She runs over to renew acquaintances with Simon, and the two furiously and simultaneously sniff and wag their tails. Sebastian deigns to lift his head up from his position on a dog bed, but decides to stay there and let Tara play the gracious hostess.

"I bring news," Corey says.

"About the case?" I'm surprised if that's true; the proper thing would be for the lawyer, in this case me, to be informed of any developments.

He grins. "I heard from administration. I have a feeling they didn't want to tell you and give you the satisfaction."

"So it's good news?" Laurie asks.

"Simon and I now have the same retirement date, and that date is today."

"That's great!" Laurie says, raising her coffee cup in a toast.

It is, in fact, great. "Biscuits are on me." I head for the biscuit jar.

When I get back, I dole them out. Even Sebastian decides they're good enough to be worth the effort it takes to chew them.

Corey turns to me. "You did a great job;

Simon and I are very grateful. I never thought you could pull it off."

"In any public fight between the bureaucracy and a dog, bet on the dog."

"Maybe so, but you played it brilliantly. How much do I owe you?"

"We've been through that already. Remember Laurie's goodness-of-my-heart speech? Besides, this one was fun."

He shakes his head. "No, I need to make this right."

"Corey . . . ," Laurie starts, but I interrupt.

"You need to make this right? It's already right. Use the money to buy Simon some designer chewies, and save a few for Tara and Sebastian. Besides, Simon was my client, not you. I'll send him a bill and he and I can work it out."

"I'm serious about this. I'm going to start doing private work, and hopefully I'll be making good money."

"I've got an idea," Laurie says. "We're starting a case."

"The Traynor thing?"

"Right. You can work on it, and your fee will cover Andy's work."

He thinks about this. "Sounds fair. What do you want me to do?"

"Too soon to know," Laurie says. "But you

can be on retainer."

I nod. "Right. We pay for your availability. If we need you, it's covered. If not, the retainer money still goes to pay off my fee. At the end of the case, we're square."

He thinks about it some, trying to decide if we're putting something over on him. Even though we might be doing just that, he buys it. "Okay, Simon and I are on call."

We're going through the motions, but it's not really possible to visit the murder scene.

Kristen McNeil's body was discovered about a hundred yards from Hinchliffe Stadium in Paterson, right near the Great Falls, a truly impressive waterfall. Hinchliffe has a storied history and is one of only two stadiums still standing in which the old Negro League baseball games were played.

But "still standing" is probably the kindest way that Hinchliffe can currently be described. It has been out of use for more than two decades and was allowed to degrade badly. Then, at the behest of the Paterson government and some influential citizens, it was declared a federal Historic Landmark, and plans were made for its restoration. There was even talk of opening a restaurant and museum on the site, as a way of generating revenue.

So far, it hasn't worked out as hoped.

Some money has been thrown at the project, most recently another $200,000 to work on the façade. But a real restoration would take more money than anyone has the stomach for, probably in the neighborhood of $25 million.

It's a worthwhile project, but Paterson has a whole bunch of more important things to do if $25 million dollars shows up. It's not like they're going to get it into the kind of shape that the Yankees would start playing their home games there. So the stadium so far has seen just cosmetic fixes, and relatively ineffective ones.

But the area has changed enough, mostly due to decay and repairs, that the scene has been substantially altered. Laurie and I always go to the murder scene first; it helps us to get a firsthand feeling for what happened. We get some information from it, but we also get an understanding that has served us well.

Unfortunately, this scene is simply not what it was when the murder happened. Too much time has passed.

It's fairly easy to tell from the police sketches where the murder took place — on the far side of the stadium, with a clear view of the Falls. To Kristen and Noah, it might have seemed like a romantic setting. But it was also desolate, and no one would have been there to help Kristen or hear her scream.

The area has not been overrun by vegetation, but there is certainly far more than the fourteen-year-old police photographs show. Back then it was basically a clearing, a logical place that the two teenagers might have chosen.

The parking lot is around at the front side of the stadium. "So they pulled up in separate cars," Laurie says. "Maybe they arrived at the same time, or maybe this was just the designated meeting place. After they argued, Noah said he left first, and he assumed she would follow."

"If she was still alive when he left, then someone else must have been here the entire time. Unless she was waiting for someone."

"I think it's most likely someone came after Noah left. They could have seen his car drive off."

"I would tend to think the other way, that someone was here already," I say. "There are plenty of places they could have been hiding where they wouldn't be seen. They could even have been within the stadium walls. If they waited for Noah's car to pull away before coming in, Kristen could have already been in her own car and leaving by then."

"But if they were here, they would have needed to leave their car somewhere. If it was in the parking lot, Noah would have seen it."

"They could have left it on the other side of the building, or in that area over there. They could have been in place before Noah and Kristen arrived, if they had advance knowledge of where they were going. Or they could have pulled up and left their car down the road; with the noise from the Falls they wouldn't have been heard."

I'm not sure that last theory is correct, because even as I'm saying it, we hear a car pulling up. Laurie reacts instantly, taking her handgun out of her purse. I just stand there, having neither of those items. I need to start carrying a purse.

But self-defense isn't needed; it's Marcus's car. He pulls up right near us and gets out, then walks around and opens the back door on the left side. He reaches in and pulls out a human being, dragging him out by the collar and resting him on the ground.

Laurie walks over to them and has a brief conversation with Marcus. I just stand there like a jerk, waiting to hear what happened and hoping that the guy on the ground is still breathing.

Laurie comes back to me. "He's the guy that's been following you; his name is Freddie Siroka. Marcus got the name by having the license plate run and has now confirmed it by checking Siroka's wallet. Marcus was concerned that we'd be out in the open here and the guy might have taken a shot at us, so he decided to terminate the surveillance."

"Is he dead?"

"No. When Marcus grabbed him, Siroka took a swing at him. Not the smartest move to make; you can see how well it worked out for him."

I nod. "Siroka might not have been class valedictorian." Then, "Are we going to wait for him to wake up so we can question him?"

She shakes her head. "You need to go home and be there when Ricky gets home from school. Marcus and I will question him. Marcus is pretty good at it. I'll fill you in when I get home."

"Works for me." This is my favorite kind of plan.

When Ricky gets home, he joins me in taking Tara and Sebastian for a walk.

Laurie comes home just as we're about to leave, and she decides to come along as well. She says she wants to stretch her legs, but she's just spent hours at the stadium, and this morning she did an hour on the exercise bike, so I've got a hunch her legs are already pre-stretched. They certainly reach the ground okay. I conclude that she wants to be around in case Siroka was not the only guy after me.

Laurie says that Marcus had something to do, but he's going to come by later to see if we have an assignment for him. Our walk takes an hour; as always, Sebastian is the reason it goes so slowly. He walks on flat terrain like he is climbing Mount Everest; if he gets any slower and lazier, I am going to have to look into getting him a canine Sherpa.

When we get home, Marcus is waiting for us on the front porch. Ricky runs ahead to give him a hug, yelling for his "Uncle Marcus." Uncle Marcus smiles and twirls him in the air before putting him down. Then Tara and even Sebastian go to Marcus to receive their petting.

I am the only living creature in the family who's petrified of Uncle Marcus.

Once we get in the house, Ricky goes to his room to pretend to do his homework while secretly watching television. Marcus, Laurie, and I go into the den so that they can update me on what they've learned. She'll be doing the updating, since she knows if Marcus does it, then I'd need subtitles or have to wait for her to tell it to me in English later on.

Laurie reveals that she and Marcus succeeded in getting Siroka to talk. He said that he was hired by a sometime associate named George Taillon to keep an eye on Andy Carpenter and to report back on where he went. No more, no less.

At first he said he had no idea of the purpose of the surveillance and that under no circumstances was he instructed to have any encounter with me. He was to meet with Taillon every other night at Taillon's apartment to give a report. His strong sense was that Taillon would then forward that report to someone else.

Under prodding, Siroka admitted that it had to do with the McNeil case, though he wouldn't go so far as to say he had knowledge of who killed her. That doesn't mean he has no such knowledge; the willingness to finger an associate is inversely proportional to the seriousness of the crime for which he is being fingered. It's one thing to say that Taillon hired Siroka to follow me; it's quite another to say he murdered an eighteen-year-old woman.

Siroka's claim that he was not to harm me in any way is consistent with his actions and also with his being unarmed when Marcus dealt with him at the stadium.

He's lucky he didn't try anything; if you're going to mess with me, you'd better be packing heat.

He might not be telling the truth and might be holding back other information, but Laurie doesn't think so. Marcus had apparently mentioned to him that if it turned out that Siroka was doing either of those things, Marcus would pay him a visit. The prospect of that would not be appealing to Siroka; I don't relish Marcus's visits and he's working for me.

Marcus had also told Siroka not to give

Taillon a heads-up that he'd spilled the beans to us, and Siroka promised not to. There is no way of telling if he will follow through on that promise. While he might not want Taillon to know that he had been busted, he'd have to tell him why he was discontinuing the surveillance.

So Siroka is faced with a decision, and based on his taking a swing at Marcus, decision-making doesn't seem to be a specialty of his.

We will commence finding out what we can about Taillon before we take our next step, but there is a good bet that he will at some point be paid a visit by me and Uncle Marcus.

"By the way," Laurie says, "I've got the whole thing on audiotape. Siroka didn't realize I was doing it; he was somewhat focused on Marcus, but if I tried to video-tape it, he would have noticed and clammed up. Will it be admissible?"

"You're worried if it's admissible?" I ask, amused.

She smiles. "You've got me thinking like a lawyer."

"That's a terrible thing to say. But we'll figure out a way to get it admitted, if we can't get Siroka to testify." It was brilliant of Laurie to tape it, and it was even legal for her to do so. New Jersey is a one-party consent state.

Our representation of Noah Traynor has obviously become a threat to someone. Until now I viewed our opposition in the case as the prosecution team and the justice system, but no way are Siroka and Taillon working for them.

Even though I am never thrilled to have enemies, in this case our discovery is potentially positive. It means another entity is out there that wants us to fail and wants Noah to be convicted.

Maybe, just maybe, that entity is the real guilty party.

That would make Noah Traynor innocent, which would in turn make Andy Carpenter happy.

Publicity definitely can cut both ways.

Whereas Simon is experiencing the glories of retirement living at least in part because of the public outcry we created, Noah is on the wrong end of the media stick.

His arrest has sparked a deluge of stories about the Kristen McNeil murder, recapturing what the feeling was like in the area back then. The justifiable fear had been that the killer would strike again, and it was a hot topic of conversation and worry.

Now everyone is being reminded of what it was like, of the horror that Kristen and her family endured, and bearing the brunt of that public reeducation will be Noah. It's fair to say that not too many of the articles and televised pieces dwell on Noah's not having been convicted of anything. They use the word *alleged* as a throwaway, as if they are checking a box.

Today I'm meeting with Jenna Silverman,

the prosecutor assigned to put Noah away for the rest of his life. I've never gone up against her before, but I'm told she is young, competent, and reasonably fair, as prosecutors go. This will be her first murder trial.

The prevailing view, and I'm sure this is held at the highest levels of the New Jersey justice system, is that Jenna's competence is unlikely to be severely tested by the upcoming trial. The prosecution's case is not complicated; Noah's DNA proves that he was there, and his not coming forward in the past fourteen years is evidence of his consciousness of guilt.

Jenna has called this meeting, and I know that the purpose is to discuss a possible plea bargain. She knows that I know that, but as is unfortunately customary in situations like this, small talk has to come first.

I hate small talk; it's small and it's talky. I wish that people were given a word budget when they are born. They can only say so many words in their life, and that's it. I would make exceptions for certain people like Vin Scully and Tony Romo and myself, but they would be few and far between.

"I'm an admirer of yours," she says. "I've studied quite a few of your cases."

I nod. "Stop it. I told myself I wouldn't cry."

"You're also a wiseass." She smiles. "I'm always surprised when I see how much judges let you get away with."

"It's because I'm extraordinarily charming. In fact, I'm about to flash my most winning smile, after which I expect you will dismiss the charges against Noah Traynor."

"Is that your way of saying I should get to the point?"

"You see right through me."

She nods. "Thirty years. No possibility of parole."

"You're way too kind."

"No, believe me I'm not. He strangled an eighteen-year-old girl; if it were up to me, we wouldn't even be having this conversation."

"What if I were to tell you that he is innocent? I would say it earnestly."

She laughs. "I'd drop the charges and throw him an apology parade."

I stand up. "I'll be the grand marshal."

"So you're taking it to trial?"

"I'll talk to my client and get back to you. But a good guess is you're going to get to watch me charm another judge."

I decide to take the offer to Noah immediately, so I head for the jail. Thirty years without parole is a horrible sentence, but life in prison is even worse, and that's what he's facing if he loses at trial. It's his call to make, and as soon as we're settled in the lawyer visiting room, I present him with his options.

He doesn't hesitate. "I can't say I'm guilty, I can't give up thirty years of my life, I can't do this to my family, all for something that I didn't do."

"You do understand that there is a very real chance you will spend the rest of your life behind bars for something that you didn't do?"

It's like I slapped him in the face; he just about recoils from my words. Then, "I know that. It's all I've been able to think about."

"You want some time to consider this? The offer will still be there next week."

"What arc our chances of winning the case?"

"If the trial was starting today, it would be zero." Conversations with clients about potential plea bargains call for absolute honesty.

"But the trial is not starting today."

I nod. "Which is why I can't predict what is going to happen. We are just starting our investigation. The difficulty is that their evidence cannot be successfully challenged.

You were there, it was your skin under her fingernails, and they can prove it.

"So while we can't prove that you didn't do it, we will need to point to someone else who might have. We're just not anywhere near that yet, and there's no guarantee that we're going to get there."

"But you're going to try? I mean, all out?"

"That I can guarantee."

He nods. "Okay. I'll think about the offer, but I know there is no way I am going to plead guilty to this."

"Fair enough."

Cynthia and Kevin McNeil have been grieving for fourteen years.

They are going to continue to grieve for the rest of their lives; nothing that happens in this trial is going to change that. That's par for the course when parents lose a child, no matter how it happens.

But the manner of Kristen's death made it even more difficult, if that's possible. It was so senseless and arbitrary, and they've had to live with the knowledge that Kristen died in abject terror with no one there to help her. Parents cannot protect their child every minute of every day, but they can sure agonize when they don't.

While someone out there truly deserved the blame, they never knew who that someone was. Until now; now they are positive it is Noah Traynor.

All of this makes perfect sense from their point of view, and it is spelled out in an interview they did last night for a local television news station. They said they would talk about this nightmare just the one time, then would have no more public comment.

They said they want Noah to get a fair trial, that they only want the real guilty party punished. But they also said that they had no interest in going to the trial because they didn't want to be in the same room as him.

Unfortunately, their claim that they would have no more public comments is actually extending to private comments, especially when it comes to us. Laurie called and asked them if we could talk with them, and they turned her down cold.

Laurie can be persuasive in situations like this; if she couldn't get them to talk, no one can. They see us as the villains who are trying to prevent their daughter's killer from having to pay for his crime. If we want to help our case by talking to them, then by definition they would refuse our request.

If I were them, I'd probably feel the same way.

Fortunately, not everyone in their family shares that point of view. Karen McNeil, Kristen's sister, took little convincing when Laurie called her. Karen is an ER nurse at

Hackensack Hospital, and she suggested we meet in the hospital cafeteria at the end of her shift.

Laurie has come along just in case the situation requires any tact or human decency. We're sitting at a table when a woman in a nurse's uniform, probably in her early thirties, walks in and surveys the room, as if looking for someone. Having seen photos of Kristen, I have no doubt who this is. Karen looks like an older version of Kristen; Kristen unfortunately never got to look like an older version of herself.

She comes over to us and asks, "Laurie?"

Laurie, always quick on her feet in conversational situations like this, answers, "Yes."

We do introductions all around, and I ask Karen if she wants anything to eat or drink. She asks for coffee, so I run off to get it. I am a vital cog in this operation.

By the time I come back, Laurie and Karen are smiling and chatting like reunited sorority sisters. We'd probably be better off if I didn't join them, but I promised her the coffee.

Laurie eventually steers the conversation toward the matter at hand. "Did Kristen ever mention Noah Traynor?"

A shake of the head. "Not to me, at least not directly."

"What do you mean, 'not directly'?"

"She said she met someone, but never said his name. I assumed she was being secretive because of Kyle."

"Kyle Wainwright?" I ask. That's the name listed in the discovery documents as Kristen's boyfriend at the time.

Karen nods. "Right. They were together for quite a while, but something was going on."

"Going on how?" Laurie asks.

"I'm not sure. But whatever it was had Kristen really upset. I figured she was dating this new guy to get back at him."

"Was he the type to react badly?" I ask.

Karen shrugs. "I guess anyone would. But Kyle wasn't the violent type; at least he didn't seem to be. I always liked him well enough. And he always seemed crazy about Kristen."

"If something was bothering Kristen, something really important, would she have been likely to confide in you? I mean, something more significant than breaking up with a boyfriend?"

Karen smiles. "Back then nothing could have been more significant than breaking up with a boyfriend. But, yeah, I think so. I was only a year younger than her, so we were close friends as well as sisters."

"Did Kristen say anything to you about leaving home?"

"No, I'd remember that. But she was doing crazy things; it was like she was going through some kind of internal crisis."

"What kind of crazy things?" Laurie asks.

"Well, for one, she quit her job. And she really seemed to like that job."

"Where did she work?"

"Some tech company; I never understood what they do. Kyle's father owned it; I think he still does. Kyle got her the job; maybe that's why she quit." Karen sighs slightly. "I never got a chance to ask her."

"Are you still in touch with Kyle?"

She shakes her head. "No. It was pretty hard even to see him after Kristen died. I think that was probably true for him as well. I heard he took it really hard, and I still haven't gotten over it. I doubt I ever will."

"We understand," Laurie says. "There's so much she could have done."

Karen nods. "Right. I might have had nieces and nephews by now." Then, "You think they have the wrong guy? How could that be?"

"We're trying to answer those questions," I say.

"It's your job to think he's innocent, right? I'm sorry, but I hope he's not; I hope he's guilty as hell."

"Why?"

"Because someone did it, and my parents need to know who that person is. So do I. Do you know they've never gone through her things? My mother cleans the room every day; she keeps it like a shrine. I'm hoping that once they know who took her away, they'll be able to move on, at least a little bit."

"They won't talk to us," Laurie says.

Karen nods. "I know. I told them they should, but got nowhere with it. I told them we have to be sure; the worst possible outcome would be for the wrong person to go to prison."

"That's exactly how we feel," Laurie says. "We don't want to cause them more pain."

"That you couldn't do. Their life ended the same day Kristen's did. They were never the same. It would be almost comical if it wasn't so awful. Do you know that someone broke into and robbed their house during the funeral? Took all my mother's jewelry. Can you imagine coming home from your teenage daughter's funeral and walking in to that?"

"No, I honestly can't," Laurie says. "Thank you for talking to us."

As we're getting up to leave, Karen asks,

"How old is your client?"

"Thirty-three," I say, since it's not exactly a state secret. "Why?

"A couple of times . . . my recollection is that it was not too long before she died . . . she asked my opinion about dating older men. I asked why she was asking, and she just shrugged it off and said she had a friend who was involved with someone. It just struck me as strange."

"Did she say anything else about it?" Laurie asks.

Karen shakes her head. "No. But if Traynor is thirty-three . . . Kristen would have been thirty-two now if she had lived."

Laurie nods. "Not much of a gap."

Charles Arrant took pride in not making strategic mistakes.

He once said that he could count the number of mental errors he had made in the previous ten years on one hand, with at least two fingers left over. But on the rare occasions when it happened, he didn't whitewash it, deny it, or avoid confronting it. He knew that only made it worse.

Instead, he fixed it. Every. Single. Time.

This time Arrant was particularly disappointed in himself. He'd overreacted to the phone call and did more than was necessary. He forced things rather than let the "game" come to him. And his move came back to bite him in the ass. That bad move could be reduced to four words: he hired a moron.

This particular moron's name was George Taillon. In Arrant's defense, he had employed Taillon before, sometimes even on significant jobs, and the results had been satisfactory. This was supposed to be a simple job, but Taillon, heretofore known in Arrant's mind as Moron Number One, had blown it by hiring Moron Number Two.

Arrant had told Taillon to watch the lawyer, Carpenter, from a distance. He was to report where he went; the information might come in handy down the road. But it wasn't crucial, and Arrant realized belatedly that it wasn't necessary at all. If Carpenter uncovered anything significant, action could be taken then.

But Taillon apparently felt the job was beneath him, and he hired Moron Number Two, Siroka. He, in turn, had blown it by allowing Carpenter to realize he was being watched. Carpenter reacted in an un-lawyer-like way by hiring muscle to deal with Siroka.

Siroka, to cement his status as a moron, had given up Taillon's name. Siroka could have given false information; Carpenter or his guy could not have known. But Siroka didn't; he got scared and gave them Taillon.

Then Siroka faced a choice. He decided that he had to tell Taillon what had happened since he could no longer do the surveillance. His dilemma was whether to admit he'd given up Taillon's name. He apparently decided, not without logic, that Taillon would find out anyway, since Carpenter was going to come after him. So Siroka told Taillon the truth.

Then Taillon faced a similar choice. He could tell Arrant what had happened or keep it from him and just restart the surveillance himself, being more careful not to be detected. Keeping it to himself would have been the smart move, since Carpenter did not have Arrant's name. All of these events might never have gotten back to Arrant.

But Moron Number One made the wrong choice. He told Arrant the truth.

The entire chain of events, Arrant knew, was not in any way devastating. Carpenter did not know about Arrant; his knowledge stopped with Taillon. The problem, though, was that it opened up a new area of investigation for Carpenter. He would be smart enough to connect it to the Traynor case and would search for the reason that someone thought it important to follow him.

All of that is why Arrant summoned Taillon to a meeting to discuss the next steps. Arrant insisted that he bring Siroka with him, so that Arrant could know all the details of what had gone down.

Taillon and Siroka arrived at the Pennington Park baseball field at eight o'clock, as instructed. Arrant was already there waiting for them, and by 8:01 the two arrivals were dead. Literally not one word had been spoken, except for "Hey!," which Siroka got out as he watched Taillon take the first bullet.

Arrant left the bodies there, so that they would be found and reported by the media. It would not stop Carpenter from investigating, but that would also have been true if Taillon and Siroka just disappeared.

So either way Carpenter would know that the new avenue of investigation had been decisively closed. And he would also know without doubt the type of person that had closed it.

The type no one wants to cross.

It's way too early for me to have any suspects.

I really don't know any of the players yet, nor do I know enough about the victim's background and associations. The sad truth is that anyone who examined the current facts would believe that the person most likely to have committed the crime is my client, although Siroka's being paid to tail me gives me actual hope that something else is going on.

But even with the little that I know, I'm interested in Kyle Wainwright, Kristen Mc-Neil's "boyfriend of record" at the time of her death. She was clearly cheating on him with Noah, and while I don't know if Kyle was aware of it, if he was, then the rejection might well have stung. He could have wanted revenge.

This brings me today to NetLink Systems, the company owned by Kyle's father, Arthur Wainwright. Arthur is what could be described as a leading citizen in North Jersey. He's politically influential nationally and is a wealthy philanthropist, donating to worthy causes through his Wainwright Foundation. I've slept through some charity dinners that he also attended, but to my knowledge we've never met.

The only other "person" I know with their own foundation is Tara, but unlike Arthur Wainwright, she keeps her charitable work low-key and doesn't seek publicity for her efforts.

Kyle works here in the Paramus headquarters. No doubt he got the job as the result of a pressure-filled interview in which he impressed the hell out of his father. I've braved a steady rain to come here to speak to him, but I haven't called ahead. I find that people find it easier to refuse an interview over the phone than face-to-face.

I ask at the reception desk to speak with Kyle, and the young woman asks if I have an appointment. When I say that I do not, she asks what it is in relation to. I tell her that I am an attorney and that it is a personal matter. I say it using my most serious grown-up voice.

She picks up the phone and tells someone that an attorney named Andy Carpenter is here asking to speak to Kyle on a personal matter. That seems to me to be a pretty accurate and succinct description of events so far.

Apparently the receptionist doesn't have too much influence around here because ten minutes go by with nothing happening. She eventually apologizes and says, "Let me call back there again," but as she picks up the phone, I hear, "Mr. Carpenter?" She puts the phone back down.

I look over and see someone who is unlikely to be Kyle Wainwright. This guy is probably in his early-to-mid-forties, which would make him a decade older than Kyle.

He approaches me with his hand extended. "My name is Jeremy Kennon. Why don't you come with me to my office?"

"I was looking for Kyle Wainwright."

He nods. "I know, but Kyle is at a meeting in the city." He smiles. "Come on back."

Since this falls under the category of "nothing to lose," I follow him back to his office. Kennon is obviously an important player here because he has an impressive corner office with all glass walls providing an unimpeded view of the surrounding area. Unfortunately, that surrounding area is not the Grand Canyon or Malibu Beach . . . it's just Paramus. When it comes to Paramus, impeded views are just as good as unimpeded ones.

"I'm head of technology here," Kennon says, "Kyle works for me; he's picked up the tech stuff very well. Obviously his father's kid."

"When will he be back?"

"Tomorrow morning. Not sure if he will want to talk to you, considering the circumstances. But he might."

"Which circumstances are you talking about?"

"You representing the guy accused of" — he hesitates — "killing Kristen," he says uncomfortably. "We're all following it pretty closely; we cared about her a lot. Hard to believe it has been so many years."

"You worked here then?"

He smiles. "Oh, yes. Fifteen years; I was one of the first employees hired."

"Has the company grown a lot over the years?"

He nods. "That's for sure. We only had two floors back then; now we have six. And every time we expand they make me switch offices; by the time I'm unpacked they're moving me again."

"Kristen McNeil worked here back then as well?" I ask that even though I know the answer.

He nods. "She did. Got here after me, but didn't stay very long. She left a week or so before she died."

"Why did she quit?"

"I'm not sure; she never told me. I came in one day and found out she was gone. I was planning to talk to her about it, but never got the chance. I don't think anyone knew; it was a mystery. But something must have happened."

"What did she do here?"

"Just assistant stuff, nothing technical. She didn't work for me, so we didn't interact that much. I think Arthur gave her the job as a favor to Kyle. But she was a hard worker, and a good kid."

"Arthur Wainwright? Kyle's father?"

Another smile. "Also known as the Big Cheese."

"What does the company do, exactly?"

"We make hardware of various kinds. Our main product is routers. Are you familiar with this stuff?"

"Absolutely. I can even tell you what a router is. It's a device that routs things."

He laughs. "You're obviously accomplished in the field. All internet communications go through routers; it directs the data . . . tells it where to go. Even internally; if I send an email to someone in the next office, it goes out into the internet world and then comes back. And routers handle all that."

"Who do you sell them to?"

"We have corporate clients, but a lot of our router production has been subcontracted to us by the huge players in the field. We're a small fish, though a profitable one."

"Is Arthur Wainwright a tech guy, or just a big-cheese guy?"

"He used to be at the top in the tech area, back when he started this company. But there are new developments every day, things change by the nanosecond, and one has to keep up with it. After a while Arthur chose to delegate to worker bees like me."

Back to the matter at hand. "Do you know what Kristen was worried about in the weeks before she died?"

He shakes his head. "No, but apparently she had good reason to worry. I just wish she had come to me, to any of us. We were a family; we still are."

"Will you ask Kyle to call me?" I hand him my card.

"I'll do that. Like I said, he might, but he might not."

"I would think he'd want to find out the truth about what happened."

"I'm sure he would. But you and Kyle might have different truths."

"Andy, come in here. Right away."

I'm in the den going over discovery documents and planning my next investigative steps. Laurie is up in bed; I thought she was reading, but based on her words, I'm hoping that she's yearning.

In any event, I've made it a lifelong habit to always obey when a beautiful woman calls me to bed, though for a lifelong habit it has happened remarkably few times.

As I reach the bedroom, I can hear that the television is on and Laurie is watching the news. The possibility of yearning being the reason for her calling me has just dropped off precipitously. But I live in hope.

"Look at this." She points to the television screen, thoroughly dashing that hope.

Two photographs are on the screen, one of which I recognize immediately. Under the two photos are the names George Taillon and Fred Siroka. I've got a hunch that they are not the subject of a piece about Nobel Prize winners.

The bodies of the two men have been found in shrubbery in Pennington Park. They were believed to have been shot to death within the past twenty-four hours; it's likely the bodies would have been discovered sooner had it not rained today. Rain cuts down on park attendance rather dramatically.

"The plot thickens," Laurie says.

"The chance that their getting shot has nothing to do with us is absolute zero," I say, as Laurie nods her agreement. "And it's safe to say we can stop looking for George Taillon."

"There are a lot of layers to this."

"What do you mean?

"Taillon paid Siroka to watch you, and it blew up in his face. A third party, we assume higher up on the chain of command, got rid of them. That's three levels, and we don't know if we reached the top yet. But if we further assume that none of the players were acting out of the goodness of their hearts, there must be serious money involved."

"All because an arrest was made in a fourteen-year-old murder," I say.

"It's what happened as a result of the arrest. Let's say that there is someone out there who is the real killer. As long as no one was charged with the crime, and as long as the police assumed whoever left the DNA was the killer, then the real guilty person was safe.

"But once Noah was arrested, then the case was once again subjected to intense scrutiny. People, more specifically us, have a reason to look into the circumstances of the murder. We are trying to find the real killer, something the real killer seems not to be pleased about."

I nod. "Real killers do look at things like that negatively."

"They do. Which is why Marcus once again has to play the role of lawyer protector. You are playing the role of lawyer in need of protection."

I shake my head. "No, not this time. At least not now. Trying to put me out of commission would put an even more intense focus on our case, which is why they won't do it. We need Marcus investigating, not protecting. Maybe that will change and we can revisit it."

"I disagree."

"I know, but this is my call. It's my name above the door."

"Your name is not above any door."

"Not a literal door. A virtual door. I can see it plain as day. It says ANDY CARPENTER, KING OF THE CASTLE."

She finally agrees, at least for now. I call Sam Willis and ask him to find out whatever he can about Taillon and Siroka.

"What are you looking for?" he asks.

"I won't know until you find it, so cast a wide net. I especially want to know if they've gotten their hands on any money recently, and where it came from."

"I'm on it."

"Wait a minute. Before you get off, tell me about NetLink Systems."

"What do you want to know?"

"What do they do? I know they make routers, and I know that all internet communications go through routers."

"Right. If not for routers, your computer would be a blank screen when you went online."

"And they sell these routers to who?"

"I don't know about them specifically, but I can take a good guess. They're a relatively small company for the field, so I would imagine that they have contracts to make them for bigger companies, and I'm sure they also have people and companies that buy from them directly."

"What else do they make?"

"A whole bunch of stuff you've never heard of. Switches, hubs, WAPs, security cameras . . ."

"I've heard of security cameras."

"Congratulations. Can I go now?"

I let him off and call Pete Stanton on his cell phone. He answers with his customary warmth: "What the hell do you want?"

"Are you at Pennington Park?" I ask, assuming that the head of Homicide would be at a double-murder scene.

"Yeah. Why?"

"I'm coming down there."

"What do you think this is, Disneyland? It's a murder scene." Then, "Why would you come down here?"

"I have information for you about the two dead guys. And you're going to give me information in return."

Pete knows me well enough to understand that I am serious about this. "Can it wait until tomorrow? I have a lot going on here and the chief just showed up."

"I'll be in your office at ten A.M."

"That will give me something to look forward to."

I hang up and tell Laurie where things stand. Then I say, "You know, when you called me in here and told me to hurry up,

140

I thought you might have been yearning for me."

"That's what you thought?"

I nod. "Yup. I didn't realize it was about two dead bodies."

"The irony is that I did initially call you because I was yearning. The dead bodies on the television were a coincidence; I only found out about them because you took so long getting here."

"I don't believe in coincidences."

"Would you be willing to make an exception just this once?"

I pretend to think about it for a few seconds. "Might as well."

Pete pushes our meeting back to 2:00 P.M.

I have no doubt that he's busy; a double murder is a big deal in cop-land. That he's seeing me at all today means he takes seriously that I have something important to say, as well as that he wants to continue to get free beer and burgers at Charlie's. Not necessarily in that order.

So I'm sitting in his office, alone, waiting for him to come back from a staff meeting. It's not until two fifteen when he walks in. "This better be good," he says. "And it better not be about the Kristen McNeil murder."

"No, you've already arrested the wrong guy in that case. I'm going to try and help you get the right guy in the double murder."

He sits behind his desk. "I can use all the help I can get."

"I'm going to want some information in return."

He frowns his disgust. "That's a first. What have you got?"

"I know how Siroka and Taillon were connected, and I've got a good guess why they were killed."

Just then a sergeant comes to the door. "The chief wants you in his office."

"Tell him I'm on something important and that I'll be there in ten minutes."

"You think I'm important?" I pretend to dab my eyes. "Have you got a tissue?"

"It was my subtle way of saying you have ten minutes. So move this along."

"Siroka had been following me; I got lucky and Marcus noticed it. Marcus interceded in typical Marcus fashion, and they got together with Laurie and chatted. I guess Siroka just considered Marcus sort of a kindred spirit, because he opened up to him. He said that Taillon had hired him to follow me, and that it had something to do with the Kristen McNeil murder."

"Interesting," Pete says.

"Have you got a pen? I want to write that down. The things you hear when you don't have a damn tape recorder."

He ignores that. "So why were they killed?"

"Because whoever hired Taillon found out that we knew about him and Siroka. Taillon may have even reported that to his bosses, since he'd have to admit that the surveillance was over. Those bosses obviously didn't trust Taillon not to reveal their identities. They didn't want me digging any further."

"Why do you think Siroka was following you?"

"Do you have hearing issues? I already told you he said it related to my case. That is supported by the fact that I took over Noah Traynor's defense just before Siroka started tailing me."

"Or maybe somebody just doesn't like you. I could give you a list."

"My turn," I say. "Had you found a connection between Siroka and Taillon?"

"They had worked together a few times; Taillon hired him for small jobs."

"Tell me about Taillon." I look at my watch. "You've got six minutes."

"He was part of a new breed that's filling the gap with the decline of mob families. He was sort of an independent contractor; gets hired on a case-by-case basis. Very good at his job. Tough guy, but clearly ran into somebody tougher."

"He worked alone?"

"That's difficult to answer. He had a loose arrangement with another guy with a similar résumé, but they were not partners."

"What do you mean by 'a loose arrangement'?"

Pete shrugs. "They'd back up each other when one couldn't handle something. Like if your dentist is out of town, you call with an emergency and he has a backup. But in this case they'd also step in to help each other when the situation required two people."

"What's the guy's name?"

"Mitch Holzer."

"Have you talked to him?"

"Yeah . . . nothing. Guys like that open up to the police all the time."

"You think he knows anything?"

"Hard to say. Following you is not exactly a job that requires an army, so I'm not sure why Taillon would have had to bring him in. But you never know."

I don't say anything, so Pete says, "If you're thinking of dealing with Holzer, think again. He is a dangerous guy, and I would say that the chance he will like you is absolute zero."

I hold up both of my hands. "You want to know what dangerous is? These hands are registered with the bar association."

"Are we done here?"

"Two more questions. When you searched

Taillon's house, did you find any money? And what about a cell phone?"

Pete looks at me strangely. "Twenty grand in cash. No cell phone, either on the body or in his house." Then he stands. "Time's up . . . thanks for coming in. It's been a real treat."

When I get home, our house is considerably more crowded than I remembered it.

That's because Ricky is having a rare, Laurie-endorsed, triple sleepover. Ricky's best friend, Will Rubenstein, is here, which is fairly common. Ricky spends a lot of time at Will's house as well, and Laurie and I are friends with Will's parents.

Also here is Danny Traynor, who at first glance seems to be fitting in quite well. The three of them are playing video games, which is why each of them holds a joystick and they do not so much as look up when I arrive.

The sleepover is a triple because Danny has brought along Murphy, his dachshund. Murphy and Tara are playing tug rope with a dog toy, while Sebastian sleeps on his bed. The three of them show about as much interest in me as the boys do.

So I walk through to the kitchen without

any reaction from anyone, human or canine. When I get there, Laurie is on the phone, so she doesn't exactly greet me with open arms either.

I wait until she gets off the call, then I say, "If a lawyer comes home and no one pays any attention, does he make a sound?"

"Are we feeling unappreciated?"

"Unnoticed."

She shakes her head. "What a tragedy. How did it go with Pete?"

I recount the conversation, and when I get to the part about Mitch Holzer, Laurie says, "I assume you're going to want to talk to him?"

"Might as well; I have to talk to somebody, and nobody around here seems interested."

"Let me have Marcus do some homework on the guy to find out what we might be dealing with. But there is someone else for you to talk to first."

"Who?"

"That phone call I was on was from Kyle Wainwright. He's expecting you at his office at ten o'clock tomorrow morning."

"Good. Hopefully he'll confess."

She smiles. "I doubt it. You think he's a viable possibility?"

"Probably not. But I'll have a better feel for it after I talk to him. It's always possible that he lost control and killed his girlfriend for cheating on him. But now, with someone hiring guys like Taillon and Siroka, this doesn't feel like that kind of situation."

She nods. "I was thinking the same thing."

"The key will be figuring out why Kristen was killed. Any chance we have rests on that."

"What do you mean?"

"Well, if the killing was random, if some violent asshole happened upon her and strangled her, we're dead in the water. We'll never find that person, and therefore we can't possibly convince a jury."

"But . . ."

"But if she wasn't killed because of bad luck, or where she was, then we have a shot. If she was killed because she was a threat to someone, because of what she knew, then at least we have hope."

Just then Ricky comes into the room. He's breathing heavily, so the video games must have been put aside and some physical playing, maybe wrestling, is going on.

"Hey, Dad, Danny says you're going to bring his father home. Can you do that?"

"We're trying, Rick. We're trying."

"I told him you'd do it, no problem."

Thanks a lot.

Sam calls and tells me that he has tracked

down the cell phone numbers for both Siroka and Taillon. That their phones are missing is not as significant to our investigation as it might seem. Everything done on a phone, and nowadays pretty much everything done in life, is recorded somewhere, by someone.

In the case of a phone, a record of all calls is stored for posterity on phone company computers. This is also true of the phone GPS records, meaning the phone company always knows where a phone is or was, even retroactively.

"I'll get right on it," Sam says. "Now that I have them."

By getting right on it, Sam means that he will hack into the phone company computers and retrieve all the information he needs. Technically, that's illegal. Nontechnically, it's also illegal. I've long ago come to terms with that, and it wasn't much of a struggle.

In my view, the absolute best thing about sleepovers are the meals. Laurie would never embarrass Ricky by serving something healthy, like salmon or, God forbid, vegetables.

So I go out and get three pizzas, ensuring enough for everyone to have a satisfying dinner, as well as leaving cold pizza for me in the morning.

These days I'm trying to appreciate the small pleasures.

I'm getting well-known here at NetLink Systems.

This time the receptionist gives me an enthusiastic hello and asks me how I am today. I decide to lie and tell her that I'm fine; it will shorten the conversation. I refer you to my previous comments about small talk.

Once again she calls back to alert Kyle Wainwright that I'm here, and this time the wait is only two minutes. The door opens and a man says, "Andy Carpenter? I'm Kyle Wainwright."

I'm momentarily surprised. I've thought of Kyle only as the eighteen-year-old boyfriend of Kristen McNeil, so it's a little jarring to see that he's in his early thirties, and even balding slightly. How come Laurie and I are the only ones who never age?

We shake hands and go back to his office, stopping to get coffee along the way. They use one of those Keurig machines, which I bought for Laurie at home, only to be told that the little pods that hold the coffee are bad for the environment when they get discarded. So the machine is sitting un-opened in a closet. If anyone wants to make an offer on it, I can get you a good deal.

Kyle's office is two doors down from that of his boss, Jeremy Kennon. Like Kennon's and all the other offices on this hallway, the walls are glass, so anyone passing by can look in. Once we're seated, I notice someone walking by who stops and looks in at us. He's about sixty years old, and what little hair he has is gray. He seems to shake his head slightly and then continues walking.

"That's my father," Kyle says.

I don't see a need to respond to that, so I don't. Instead I ask, "So, you've had four-teen years to think about it. Any idea who killed Kristen McNeil?"

He shakes his head. "No, like everybody else I've always assumed it was whoever left their DNA on the scene." Then, "Man, it seems so long ago, like in another lifetime. But it also seems like it was yesterday."

"I understand that she had broken up with you shortly before she died?"

"Not officially. She just wanted space, needed time to think, that kind of stuff. But that's the kind of thing they always say, you know? I've used those lines a few times myself. But, yeah, whatever the reason, the handwriting was on the wall. But it wasn't final, or at least I didn't think so."

"But she quit her job here; that seems somewhat final."

He nods. "I remember being surprised by that. We didn't work in the same department, and even if she dumped me, it wasn't like she was going to get fired. My father liked her, and I never would have been vindictive like that. We were really young. But those were strange times."

The phone on Kyle's desk rings. He can't see it from where he's sitting, but makes no effort to answer it.

"You want to get that?"

He shakes his head. "It's my private line, which means it's my wife. I'll call her back, and she'll remind me to pick up something at the market on the way home."

"How long have you been married?"

"Four years. One child, three years old. I won't force you to see pictures of her, but take it from me, she's adorable."

I'm sure I'm supposed to insist on seeing the pictures, but I don't. "You were away the day Kristen was killed?"

"Yeah . . . hey, wait a minute, you think I

might have killed her?"

"I don't have the slightest idea. Do the names Freddie Siroka or George Taillon mean anything to you?"

He thinks for a moment. "No . . . should they?"

I was searching for a reaction — and got none. Which of course means absolutely nothing. "Did you know Noah Traynor?"

"Your client? No, never met him, and Kristen never mentioned him to me. The first I heard of him was when they announced the arrest." Then, "Look, if you're trying to make a case that I killed Kristen, or even got someone else to do it, you're really wasting your time. Although I guess I'd be saying that even if I did it."

"I'm just covering all the bases, but thanks for answering my questions."

The door opens and a young woman peers in. "Mr. Carpenter, Mr. Wainwright would like to talk to you before you leave."

"Uh-oh . . . that's my father," Kyle says. "You're going to get sent to your room without supper."

The woman smiles at what I guess is a common joke around here. "If you're ready, you could just follow me. . . ."

So I do. I follow her to the office all the way down the hall to the other corner office, on the opposite side of Kennon's. But Arthur Wainwright's office makes Kennon's and Kyle's look like telephone booths, if telephone booths still existed.

The woman knocks on the door, then opens it. Arthur Wainwright looks up from his desk as if annoyed, which seems unusual since he requested the meeting. He calls me in with a hand motion, and in the reverse motion seems to dismiss the woman. This guy is good with his hands.

"I want you to leave my son alone," he says.

"Fine, thanks, how are you?"

"I mean it. He's been through enough."

"We had a conversation; no threats and no punches thrown. He seemed like he came out of it pretty well. But if you're worried, I'll send him some flowers. What's his favorite color?"

"I know all about you, Carpenter."

"You do? Then what's my favorite color?"

"Get out of here."

"You just asked me to come in. Are you rescinding your invitation?"

"Leave now."

"Your son is a grown man. What are you so afraid of?"

"Would you like me to have you thrown out?"

"Believe me, I've been thrown out of better places by better people," I say as I leave. It's a pretty good exit line and would be even better if it weren't true.

Gale Halpern was Kristen McNeil's best friend.

At least that's how she was characterized in a number of media stories at the time of Kristen's death, as well as in many of the follow-up stories since. She wasn't talking to the press in the weeks following the crime, but she's given a couple of interviews in recent years.

Laurie has tracked her down and she agreed to talk to me. She asked that I come to her house, which is on Morlot Avenue in Fair Lawn. When I pull up, she comes out on the porch to greet me, shaking my hand with her right hand while cradling a baby girl in her left arm. At least I'm guessing it's a girl; the blanket is pink.

We go inside and I almost trip over a small tricycle in the hallway. "I don't think she's ready for this yet."

Gale laughs. "I don't think so either. That

belongs to Bobby; he's my oldest. He's almost seven."

"Sounds like there's more than two?"

She nods. "Chris . . . Christine . . . is three."

This woman has her hands full, quite literally. It also once again highlights the terrible loss that occurred when her best friend died; Kristen might have gone on to bring other people into the world or cure some disease or just do kind things for people that needed kindness.

I am Andy Carpenter, sentimentalist.

"It's so hard to believe it's been fourteen years." Gale points to a photograph in a frame on the mantel of two teenage girls, arms draped over each other's shoulders, mugging for the camera. "That's how I'll always remember her because that's how she'll always be."

"Do you know why she was running away?"

"Who said she was running away?"

It's not a good sign that I know more about Kristen McNeil's mind-set than the person I'm interviewing. "People who knew her."

Gale shrugs. "I knew her as well as anyone, and she never told me that. But if it's true, then I would think she was getting away from Kyle."

"She was afraid of him?"

Gale nods. "I don't mean physically; he never hit her or anything. But he was taking over her life and she was feeling confined. He wanted to know where she was all the time; I think that's why he got her the job at his father's company."

"Did you know Noah Traynor?"

"Not by name, but I knew there was somebody."

"Why?"

"I never said this before, but I think she was having an affair . . . although I guess at that age 'affair' sounds too sophisticated. She was fooling around, but she thought she was in love."

"But you don't know with who?"

"No, she wouldn't say, which was unlike her. We talked about everything, or at least I thought so. But people keep secrets."

"Do you think Kyle knew about it?"

"I don't know for sure, but I'd bet he did. He knew every move she made. He was incredibly possessive."

"Were you surprised when she quit her job?"

Gale nods. "Very. She loved that job and she really loved earning money. Kristen spent money faster than anyone I've ever known; she just loved to shop. She was making good money at her job, but was still borrowing from me.

"Kristen always wanted to be older than she was; she was in a hurry to get somewhere, but I don't think she knew where. She seemed to think she'd know when she got there."

"Was she interested in dating older men?" Kristen's sister had said her impression was that Kristen might have been doing just that.

Gale almost does a double take. "How did you know that?"

"That's a yes?"

Gale nods. "She talked about it a lot. I don't know if she actually dated anyone older, but the idea certainly appealed to her."

"If she loved her job, why would she have quit?"

"I wish I could help you. Maybe you're right; maybe she was running away. But she had a life here, and family, and friends, and a job. If she was leaving all that, then something bad must have happened. Maybe the guy she was having the affair with dumped her. But I would say she was not running towards something; she was running away from something."

There's nothing more for me to learn

from Gale, which is just as well, because she tells me that it's diaper-changing time.

All in all, nothing that Gale said to me is positive for us, and it would likely be negative in the eyes of the jury. If Kristen was having a secret affair, then the most likely person she was having it with would be the guy she rendezvoused with outside Hinchliffe Stadium.

My only suspect, and it's a stretch to even use that word, is Kyle Wainwright. Regardless of who Kristen might have been fooling around with, the result was that she was clearly separating from Kyle.

That would give him reason to be angry and lash out, particularly if he was as controlling as Gale makes him out to be. But he was out of town that day; that seems incontrovertible.

Do eighteen-year-old boys have the resources and connections to hire hit men? What about if they have rich fathers?

My next stop is the Coach House Diner on Route 4 to talk with Steven Halitzky, Kyle's college roommate at Tufts. I've caught a break in that Halitzky lives in Short Hills and works in the city, so it was not inconvenient for him to stop here on the way home.

I'm sitting in a booth having coffee when

he walks in, looks around the large restaurant, and comes right over to me. "How ya doing?" he asks, smiling.

"How did you know who I was?"

"Are you kidding? I've seen you on television a bunch of times. You're a celebrity."

I like this guy already. He sits down and orders coffee and an English muffin. We chitchat a bit and he tells me that he is the creative director at a Manhattan ad agency. "This is the first day this month I've been out of the office before eight o'clock." Then, with a grin: "You're my excuse."

"Happy to do it. Have you stayed in touch with Kyle Wainwright?"

He shakes his head. "No, we see each other occasionally at get-togethers related to the school, but that's it. We were roommates as freshmen in the dorm, but then we both got apartments off campus. We weren't that close, which is a nice way of saying I didn't like him very much. I don't think he was crazy about me either. We weren't enemies or anything; we just had different interests and attitudes about things."

"Did he talk about the murder of his girlfriend, Kristen McNeil?"

Halitzky nods. "A few times, maybe more than a few."

"Do you remember what he said?"

"Well, first of all, he said she was his ex-girlfriend, that they had broken up."

"So he wasn't terribly upset?"

"If he was, he hid it pretty well. And it sure didn't stop him from dating and partying. I'm talking about right out of the gate."

"Anything else you can tell me about him? Whether it relates to Kristen McNeil or not. I'm trying to get an accurate picture of who he is."

"I'll tell you one thing: I think it's hilarious that he wound up working for his father."

"Why?"

"He hated the guy. Talked about him like he was the worst father of all time; all he cared about was money and looking good. Apparently he used his high-priced lawyers to screw Kyle's mother in the divorce and left them with basically nothing."

"What brought Kyle and his father back together?"

Halitzky grins. "You tell me. You think money was involved? All I know is that Kyle said his father's whole public persona, the charity stuff and everything, was a fake. That behind closed doors his father was . . . well, one time he called him a 'piece of garbage.' "

We talk some more, but I don't learn

anything that seems significant. I thank Halitzky for coming, pay the check, and we both go our separate ways. I got some information today, about both Kristen McNeil and Kyle Wainwright. Like all information that I acquire during an investigation, it might someday prove useful, or not.

I'll know when I know.

As Thanksgivings go, this one is more crowded than usual.

Laurie has invited Julie and Danny Traynor to join us, and they've brought Murphy, the dachshund. Tara has definitely taken a liking to Murphy, and they sort of wrestle and sniff each other a lot. I think Sebastian likes him and is excited to see him too, because a couple of times he's summoned up the energy to blink.

Sam Willis is also going to join us, though he won't be here until almost mealtime. My major focus is how to arrange it so that I get to watch the most football possible, a job made easier by Laurie's being great about stuff like that.

The Traynor contingent arrived at ten thirty this morning, at my suggestion. I thought it would be fun for Danny to go down to the Tara Foundation to see all the rescue dogs. We have twenty-five there at all times; as we place them in homes, we just rescue more to take their place.

So Danny, Ricky, Tara, Murphy, Sebastian, and I head down there. We're a little delayed because getting Sebastian up into the back of an SUV would ordinarily require a construction crane. But with Laurie's and Julie's help, I manage it, and we're off.

Willie Miller and his wife, Sondra, are waiting for us, even though the foundation is closed today. It is remarkable how much they love doing this, and I very much appreciate how they don't begrudge my putting in so many fewer hours than they do, especially when I'm on a case.

Willie lets all the dogs out into the main play area, and Ricky, Danny, Murphy, and Tara dive right into the middle of it. If it is possible to have more fun than they do for a full hour, I'd like to see it. I'm exhausted from watching them.

Doing this was a great idea, especially since football doesn't start until twelve thirty. It even briefly takes my mind off the fact that I am making no progress in avoiding a lifetime in jail for Danny's father. Emphasis on the word *briefly* . . .

We head back home, and Sam comes over in time to watch the Lions play the Packers. Ricky and Danny start to watch with us, but then Ricky suggests that they stop watching the television to go out in the backyard and play.

Where did I go wrong?

We eat the meal between games. It's so good that I don't even mind missing the first few minutes of the Redskins-Eagles game. Laurie has always been a great cook, but with Julie helping her, she has scaled new heights.

After dinner Sam and I head to the game, and at half-time he asks, "Did you get my email?"

"No; what email is that?"

"I tried to call you, but you were out investigating something and you had your phone off. So I emailed some stuff to you."

I shake my head. "I stopped in the office, but my computer was down; the wireless wasn't working."

"That's what happens when your internet provider owns a fruit stand."

Sam has long been on my case for using the wireless that Sofia Hernandez provides. It's always been good enough for me, except for the times it doesn't work, which is too often. Sam, though his office is in the same building, has his own network.

I vow that I'll change the setup, but we both know that I won't. It's too much trouble and involves too much technical stuff that I don't want to deal with. Besides, when my imminent retirement is official, I won't even keep the office.

"Should I open the email from here now, or can you summarize?"

"Open it when you get a chance, there's a lot of detail in there. But I can tell you a couple of highlights if you want me to."

"Please."

"Okay. Taillon didn't use his cell phone much, so it wasn't hard to track the calls down. I went back twenty years; that's as long as the phone company keeps records. He kept the same number down through the years, so that made it even easier. I'm sure he switched hardware a bunch of times."

Sam tends to take forever to get to a point. "Sam, can we move this along? Halftime is almost over."

"Okay. There are twenty-one calls that he received from eighteen different burner phones. As best I can tell, they were purchased, used maybe a few times, and never used again. I can't trace who owned them."

"Makes sense. I'm sure he dealt with people that didn't want to be traced."

Sam nods. "Right. But two of the calls were made the day before Kristen McNeil's murder, and one that night."

"Are you sure?" I ask unnecessarily, since in matters like this Sam is always sure, and always right.

"Yes. They were made from three different phones. If it's one person making the calls to him, he is a very careful guy."

This is stunning news, and it leads to a few conclusions. For one thing, Taillon's hiring Siroka to follow me clearly relates to the Noah Traynor case. Siroka had said that, but this confirms it. For another, Taillon was probably himself involved in Kristen McNeil's murder, whether directly or indirectly.

And last, it makes perfect sense that Taillon was killed, maybe by his own employer. He obviously knew a great deal, and we knew about him. He therefore presented an intolerable risk.

"This is significant stuff, Sam. Thanks."

"You want the other highlight?"

"There's more?"

He nods. "A week before Kristen McNeil was murdered, Taillon placed two calls to NetLink Systems."

This case is different from most.

In almost every situation in which a defendant is accused of murder, the defense has certain standard options. Credibility of witnesses can be called into question, alibis can be offered, prosecution theories can be attacked.

In this case? Not so much.

The prosecution will confidently offer their DNA evidence and dare us to knock it down. They will say, without fear of contradiction, that Noah Traynor was at Hinchliffe Stadium with Kristen McNeil and that she had his skin fragments under her fingernails.

They will also say, again without fear of contradiction, that he could not have missed media reports about the murder, yet did nothing. Did not come forward, did not explain himself, did not offer to help, did not submit to questions . . . nothing.

They have no fear of contradiction because we cannot contradict them. We can try to attack the science, but time and time again that has proven to be futile. We can attack the way the police got to Noah through the online DNA site that initially sent them to his brother. But that issue, adjudicated in other venues, has been determined to violate no privacy rights.

We can attack the forensic people that collected it: we can claim they were incompetent or corrupt or that they screwed up the chain of custody. But if I get up in court and do any of that, everyone within the sound of my voice will know I am full of shit.

Simply put, the prosecution is right; Noah was there, he did leave those skin fragments behind, and he never subsequently came forward in fourteen long years. They don't have to offer theories; they simply have to present that evidence and let the jury decide.

With this fact pattern, there is no question how they would decide. Which means we cannot attack this head-on, so we have to come at it through a side door, and when we come in that door, we had damn well better have with us a person we can point to as the real murderer.

The only people that I know now that could possibly fit this description are Siroka and especially Taillon. The bad news is that they are not going to be walking through that door because they are both dead.

To make matters significantly worse, it will be much harder to investigate Taillon and Siroka now that they have moved on to the great beyond. I assume that someone found that to be a motivating factor when deciding to kill them.

So while I am fairly certain that Taillon and maybe Siroka are directly connected to the McNeil killing, I am nowhere close to getting an impartial observer to believe it.

I can't even pin down who Taillon called at NetLink Systems. It could have been Kyle; maybe he hired Taillon to kill Kristen when Kyle was out of town and therefore had an alibi. Or it could have been any other employee there. Kristen worked there and obviously knew a lot of people in the place, so there is no telling who had a reason to want to hurt her.

It is not even inconceivable that Taillon could have called Kristen herself. Her sister indicated that Kristen might have been having an affair with an older man; maybe she had taken up with Taillon. He was a dangerous guy, so something could have happened that made her scared and want to leave town.

Which brings us to Mitch Holzer. He's the guy that Pete Stanton said was a semi-associate of Taillon's, the person who would back up or fill in for Taillon when Taillon needed help or was unavailable. Pete described him as an independent contractor, much like Taillon, and said to be careful with him, that he was dangerous.

Laurie has had Marcus checking Holzer out and figuring out the best way to approach him. I already know that the best way to approach him is while standing behind Marcus, but I'm willing to listen to suggestions. He has just called to report in and is on the phone with Laurie offering those suggestions.

Laurie does almost no talking on the call, again simply offering a few *Okay*s and *Right*s. This compares to when I talk to Marcus; the only words I say are *What?* and *Huh?*

When she finally gets off, she says, "Marcus is going to take you to see Holzer tonight."

This is not pleasant news; I don't like putting myself into dangerous situations, even though it always seems to happen. My instinct is always to delay it as much as possible. "Tonight? I have plans for tonight."

"What kind of plans?"

"I was hoping to have dinner with my family, so that we could discuss family stuff."

"Family stuff?"

"Right. Like how was your day, how was Ricky's day, how was my day. That's what families do; they talk at dinner about their day. Then I was going to help with the dishes, and there's a really good *Seinfeld* rerun on. It's the one where George sleeps with the cleaning lady at work."

"I'll DVR it for you."

"It's not the same. I like to watch it live."

"It was shot twenty years ago. Should I tell Marcus you don't want to talk to Holzer?"

She's got me; she knows that even though my cowardice is shining through in bright neon, I'll have to go. If I refused, I'd be letting down my client. This represents a perfect example of why I don't like to have clients in the first place.

"I'll go. But make sure Marcus knows that he has to stop Holzer from killing me."

This isn't necessarily going to be so bad.

Holzer is supposed to be a dangerous guy; I'll take that as a given. But I am only going to talk to him. If he refuses, he refuses, but he can do so without resorting to violence.

On the other hand, it's not exactly breaking news that many people find me annoying. I have seen enough examples of it to know that on some level it must be true. If it walks and annoys like a duck, it's a duck.

If Holzer is one of those people, and there's a good bet that he will be, then things could get a bit scary.

Enter Marcus Clark.

Marcus picks me up at the house at 10:00 P.M. Laurie kisses and hugs me good-bye; she claims she's not worried, but I don't quite get that display of affection when I go to Charlie's to have burgers and beer with Vince and Pete.

We drive to a bar on Market Street in

downtown Paterson. The area is known for having its share of violent crime; the only way I would ordinarily come down here at this hour would be if I was accompanied by a Marine battalion, or Marcus.

Laurie said that Marcus told her that Holzer hangs out in this bar pretty much every night and actually uses an office in the back. I come up with a strategy on the way down there and share it with Marcus. He doesn't respond, doesn't even say anything, but I have to assume he's heard me because I'm sitting about three feet away from him and the radio is off.

The plan is not terribly complicated. Marcus is going to go in first and situate himself in a place from which he can observe. I'm then going to approach Holzer and try to talk to him, without his realizing that Marcus and I are together. I don't want Holzer to see me as an enemy, but good buddies don't bring Marcus Clark to a meeting.

We park a few stores down from the bar, and Marcus goes in while I wait in the car. This means that I will have to walk about fifty feet by myself, which does not please me. But I give him about three minutes, then take a deep breath and follow.

Probably fifteen people are in the bar, and the first complication is that I have no idea what Holzer looks like. I could yell, *Hey, Holzer!,* and see who turns around, but instead I go over to the bartender, who looks at me like I'm from another planet. Which I guess I am.

"I'm looking for Holzer," I say.

The bartender doesn't say a word, much like Marcus in the car. My words have no impact on these people; you'd think they were on a jury. All the bartender does is turn and go through a door to the back. Hopefully Holzer is back there and he's going to come out and talk to me.

About three minutes later the bartender returns and says, "He'll meet you in the back in five minutes."

"Through that door?" I point to the door the bartender just used.

He shakes his head. "No. Around the back. Through the alley."

I think I see the bartender make eye contact with a guy near the end of the bar. A large guy, by appearance he would fit the dictionary definition of goon. The combination of him and the word *alley* is somewhat worrisome. But I say, "Okay . . . thanks . . . five minutes," to the bartender.

In the meantime, the goon gets up, noticeably does not make any effort to pay for his drink, and goes outside. I walk over near

Marcus and whisper, "He told me to meet Holzer in the back of the alley in five minutes. I think the guy that just left is involved."

Marcus doesn't say anything; he just gets up and leaves. I hope he's not going home; I wish I had kept the car keys.

I wait the five minutes, which seems like five seconds, then I take a deep breath and go outside. The alley is to the right of the bar, and I instruct my legs to continue walking into the alley and toward the back of the building.

I am almost there when a figure appears next to me, not saying anything but walking at my side. It's Marcus, which is good news.

We turn the corner, and dim but decent light is coming from various windows in the adjacent buildings. Standing against the building are two men, the goon from the bar and another large guy I assume is Holzer.

The goon says to me, "Just you." Then, to Marcus: "Beat it."

Holzer, if that's who it is, says, "Oh, shit."

Marcus, in typical Marcus fashion, does not say anything and does not move.

"I told you to beat it," the goon says.

"That's Marcus Clark, right?" Holzer asks no one in particular.

"I don't care who it is," says the goon, who will now and forever be known as the *idiot goon.*

The idiot goon makes a move toward Marcus, I assume to attempt to physically remove Marcus from the premises. The idiot goon reaches out with his arm, and Marcus takes that arm, sort of pivots around, and emulates an Olympic hammer throw, using the idiot goon as the hammer.

In the dim light the result is a little hard to see, but the sound echoing through the mostly enclosed area is crystal clear. The way Marcus performed the act, one can't say which part of the idiot goon's body hit the brick wall first. Based on the crunching sound, and that he just crumples to the cement unmoving, I'm thinking it was his head.

"I tried to warn him," Holzer says.

"You and Marcus have met?" I ask.

Holzer nods. "Once, from a distance. But he's a known quantity. You I don't know."

"So why did you set up this scene back here?"

He shrugs. "Somebody comes looking for me, I'm careful. Especially after what happened to G."

Taillon's first name was George, so I'm assuming that's who he's talking about. But

I ask him, just to be sure, and he confirms it.

"Who killed him?" I ask.

"I still don't know who the hell you are."

"My name is Carpenter; you can call me C. I'm a lawyer, and Taillon hired someone to follow me. His name was Siroka and they both got killed. I want to know who wanted me followed and why. I think that person is the same one that killed Taillon and Siroka."

"I don't know anything about why you were being followed, nor do I give a shit."

I nod. "I didn't ask you that. I asked you who killed Taillon."

"I want to get the son of a bitch as much as you do. I got the word out on the street."

"Good. So what is the son of a bitch's name?"

Holzer thinks for a few moments, as if coming to a decision. The only sounds I hear are the small groans coming from the idiot goon. Marcus looks over at him; he seems to be at least partially awake and taking in the scene, but doesn't seem inclined to get up and back in the action.

Finally Holzer says, "I could be wrong; I'm just making a guess here."

This is like pulling teeth. "Guess away."

"There's a name, a guy, that's hired G a few times in the past. I heard his name once. But when he called, G would drop everything. He wouldn't tell me anything about the guy; he let the name slip by accident. I guess he didn't want me to horn in on the action, which meant the guy paid big money. G wanted to keep it for himself."

"What was the name?"

"Not long ago, I had a job that I needed some help on, but G bailed on me. He said he had a job, and he couldn't take anything else on. I had the feeling that the same guy was using him for something."

This is taking forever; I'm tempted to have Marcus beat it out of him. "What is the guy's name?"

"You didn't hear it from me, right?"

I nod; we could be getting close. "Right."

"Arrant. The guy's name is Arrant."

I've never heard the name Arrant, which is not significant.

Plenty of bad guys are not on my radar, which is fine with me.

That might not even be the guy's name. Holzer said he only heard it once, so it could have been slightly different. It also wouldn't have seemed terribly important to Holzer at the time, so he might be mis-remembering it. And even if he got it mostly right, it could be spelled a few different ways.

Holzer didn't provide a first name. Who knows, maybe Arrant *is* the guy's first name. Maybe it's Arrant Smith. Or Arrent Ramirez. Or Aaron Schwartz.

But the good news is that I have a number of ways to check it out, the first one being Sam Willis. So Sam is the first call I make as soon as I get home, even though it's almost midnight. Sam is always awake.

Uncharacteristically, he sounds out of it when he answers the phone, so I ask, "Did I wake you?"

"No. I've got the flu; damn thing is wiping me out."

"Sorry to hear that. If you're up to it, call me tomorrow."

"Is this about a case? Tell me now; I need something to take my mind off how bad I feel."

I tell him about the name Arrant and how I need whatever information Sam can find. I would give him more details, but I don't have any.

"I'm on it. If I come up with anything, I'll email you a report. I don't want to come over and risk you guys catching this, and it hurts my throat to talk."

Depending on what Sam can come up with, I might go to Pete Stanton or Cindy Spodek, our friend at the FBI, to further dig up information on whoever this Arrant guy might be. He's our only lead now, which doesn't say much for the status of our investigation.

The morning starts on a decidedly down note; Hike comes over to go over pretrial preparation. He's written and we've filed a series of briefs, such as change of venue, request for bail, inadmissibility of certain evidence, et cetera. We're doing it now because we've come into the case late, and some of them basically duplicate efforts that the public defender had already made.

We've put a new twist on them, but it's not going to matter. Some of them have already been rejected, and the rest will be. If we're going to have any success in this case, it's going to have to be in front of the jury.

We've tracked down a few people that we can use as character witnesses for Noah, but it's basically fluff to pad our case. Our basic problem remains: we are not going to be able to prove Noah innocent; we must show that someone else is possibly guilty.

It's all depressing, so much so that Hike's leaving doesn't even make me feel better. I'm going to spend the rest of today rereading the discovery documents and reviewing witness statements.

To break up the pain of that, I'm also going to head down to the Tara Foundation for some dog therapy and pick Ricky up from school. But even with those welcome respites, it looks like it's going to be a long and uneventful day.

Once again, I'm wrong. A major event happens in the form of a phone call from Sam Willis. His voice is still raspy from his illness as he says, "I can't believe you haven't called me."

At first I think he means I should have checked in to find out how he's feeling, but that's not really Sam's style. "Why should I have called you?"

"Why? The email I sent after we talked last night. It took me all of twenty minutes to research. What did you think?"

"I just checked my emails. Didn't get anything."

"I sent it to your work email."

"Oh, I checked personal. You want to tell me about it?"

"You should look at it and call me back. But it's huge."

I hang up and open my business email account, which I obviously don't need to be in the office to access, and which I almost never check. After all, I work as little as possible. Sure enough, there's an email from Sam:

"The guy Holzer was talking about is Charles Arrant. He was born in London, but has lived all over the world. But get this . . . there's an Interpol Red Notice Alert out on him. In fact, there are three of them. I've attached a bunch of documents. Call me. Sam."

Even before I download the documents, I

know that Sam is already right about one thing: this is huge.

Somehow Sam has gotten access to the actual Interpol documents, as well as media reports and other background information. But it all boils down to Arrant's having gotten Red Notices at the request of three countries: Great Britain, France, and Sweden. A number of photographs of him are also included, to help law enforcement around the world identify him.

What that means is that international arrest warrants are out on him. Any country that is part of the system can detain and arrest Arrant, after which he would be extradited to one of the three named countries.

But the background information makes it clear that Arrant's transgressions are not limited to those three countries. He is an international pariah, and the crimes he is alleged to have committed range from murder, to financial frauds of various types, to espionage. He is rumored to be financed by Chinese interests, but nothing here proves that.

The real stunner is that these Red Notices are more than ten years old; Arrant has not been seen in all that time.

I need to keep reminding myself that he is connected to our case by the most fragile of threads. All we have on him is the name given to us by Holzer. Even if this is the same guy that Holzer was talking about, that Taillon was working for at one point, there is not even close to a guarantee that it has anything to do with Kristen McNeil's murder.

The question I ask myself is, Why would an international criminal want to kill an eighteen-year-old girl in Paterson, New Jersey?

And my answer, unfortunately, is, Beats the shit out of me.

"You know anything about this?"

The voice asking the question belongs to Pete Stanton. He's calling at seven o'clock in the morning as I'm about to take Tara and Sebastian on their morning walk. I can hear the whirring sound of Laurie on the stationary bike in the exercise room.

If Pete is calling at this hour, it's not to ask why the Giants attempted a field goal rather than going for a first down on fourth and one last week. This is clearly work related, to probably both his work and mine.

"What are you talking about?"

"It's all over the news."

"I just woke up, Pete. I don't dream the news."

"Mitch Holzer is dead."

"Damn . . . murdered?"

"Unless you would describe a bullet in his brain as natural causes. Of course, if your client was the shooter, you probably would."

This is stunning news and it immediately registers in my brain as a confirmation of sorts that Arrant is our guy.

No coincidences.

Even though people are demonstrating a disturbing tendency to get killed after meeting me, this one can't be my fault. Holzer was the one out looking for Arrant; somehow Arrant must have found that out.

"Why are you calling me, Pete?"

"Because I told you about Holzer and now he's dead. I'm guessing you have information about it."

"I might." I'm not prepared to decide in the moment how much I want to share with Pete; I have to first calculate whether I would be helping or hurting my client's position by doing so. "But as you know, I am notoriously tight-lipped."

"Let's hear it."

"I'll come in later this morning."

He's not happy about it, but we arrange for me to be down at the precinct at eleven o'clock. Then I tell Laurie what has happened, and she finds the news important enough to cut her exercise bike ride short.

We turn on the television to learn what we can about Holzer's death. His body was found lying next to his car in a parking lot down the street from the bar where I spoke to him. He took one bullet in the back of the head, execution-style.

Holzer was no amateur; if Arrant took him out so easily, then Arrant's reputation is well justified.

"And he's obviously worried about something," Laurie says. "If he did this, and I would say it's likely that he did, then he killed Taillon, Siroka, and Holzer all to keep something quiet."

"Not necessarily. Taillon and Siroka, yes. But Holzer said that he was putting the word out about Arrant. Arrant has been invisible for ten years; he's got countries after him. Maybe he just didn't want any scrutiny at all. Although I don't know how Arrant could have such street connections in Paterson that he found out about Holzer. According to Holzer, they had no direct contact."

"So you think it's possible that Holzer's death could have nothing to do with our case?"

"All of it could have nothing to do with our case. We're just making educated guesses and hoping."

"You don't mean that."

I nod. "You're right, I don't."

We talk about how much I should be telling Pete about what I know, and then Laurie expresses concern for my safety, since I had spoken to Holzer and learned Arrant's name. Knowing Arrant's name seems to reduce one's life expectancy.

I tell Laurie that I'm not worried, that for Arrant to go after me would bring huge publicity and unwanted attention to him. Besides, I don't know anything of consequence, so I'm not a threat to him, at least not at this point.

I head downtown for my meeting with Pete, who starts the conversation by saying, "We've got a lot of people getting shot around here. And you seem to be hovering over all of it."

"I do what I can."

"So tell me about Holzer."

"After you mentioned him as being Taillon's backup, I went to talk to him."

"Where?"

"At the bar where he hangs out on Market Street. I was there the other night."

"You went down there to talk to Holzer? You?"

An insult is implied there, but I ignore it. "Marcus," I say.

Pete nods. "We had a report that a muscle guy that worked for Holzer wound up in the hospital with a busted skull."

I nod. "I think Marcus happened upon

him after he fell. He tried to catch him, but he was a moment too late."

"I'll bet. Go on."

"I asked Holzer if he had any idea who killed Taillon and Siroka because I think it is all about the Noah Traynor case. I believed that whoever had hired Taillon to have me followed also had him killed when I found out about it."

Pete frowns his disagreement at this, but doesn't interrupt, so I continue, "He didn't know, but he had an idea. And the idea had a name."

"And the name was?"

"Arrant. That's all he knew. Arrant. He said he had put the word out on the street to find the guy, but so far had no luck."

"Arrant," Pete repeats, as if trying to figure out if the name had any meaning to him. It doesn't seem to. "That's a last name?"

"It is; look him up. If it's the same guy, he's wanted by more countries than you could place on a map."

"What does that mean? Interpol?"

"You're not as dumb as you look."

"I'll check this out."

I hand Pete copies of the documents that Sam got for me, including the official ones from Interpol. He looks at me with suspicion. "Where did you get these?"

"From the international criminal fairy."

He looks at the documents for a while. "What the hell is this guy doing here?"

"He's covering up something big that's been going on for a long time. And it's got to be more than just the murder of Kristen McNeil."

Pete nods. "Okay, you've given me the information. What's the quid pro quo?"

"What do you mean?"

"I mean what do you want from me?"

"I want you to catch him."

The truth is that the Paterson Police have no chance of getting Arrant.

That's not even a criticism of them. If the entire world has been looking for him for a decade, he's not about to let himself get nabbed by a Jersey police department.

It's even questionable whether catching him would help us. He doesn't sound like the type to wilt and tell all because the cops are shining a hot light on him. And he'd probably be in custody for about twenty minutes before the FBI would come in and take him away. We'd have as much access to him then as we do now.

We're going to somehow have to connect him to our case without physically having him, or talking to him. I just wish I knew how.

With Holzer, Taillon, and Siroka out of the way, Arrant may even have already left the area. This does not sound like a guy who overstays his welcome; for all I know he could be in Lithuania by now.

I am interested in how he came to view Holzer as a danger. I understand that Holzer had been asking around about him, but Holzer was a local street guy whose base of operations was a downtown bar. Somehow Arrant must have been tied into that world, enabling him to access information, as unlikely as it may seem.

"Maybe we should call Cindy Spodek," Laurie suggests after dinner, and after Ricky has gone to his room to do homework. Cindy is an FBI agent, number two in the Boston Bureau, who we have exchanged information with in the past. She's a good friend of Laurie's and a semi-good friend of mine.

"Maybe . . . let me think about it," I say.

"What's the downside?"

"It could set off a chain reaction that would make Arrant aware that we know about him. I doubt he could know that Holzer mentioned his name to us, so he would have no reason to see us as a threat."

"I disagree. Remember, he's the one who most likely ordered Taillon to get you followed."

I nod; she has a point. "Okay. Let me think about it. Maybe we'll call Cindy tomorrow. For now I need to walk and think."

She knows what I mean: I do my best thinking, such as it is, while walking Tara and Sebastian in the park. "I still think we should have you protected; just in case," she says.

I'm always torn in situations like this. I want to be protected, because it feels very protective. But I never want to admit it, especially to Laurie. Which is ridiculous, since she knows better than anyone that I am totally unable to protect myself. "I'll think about it," I finally say.

So Tara, Sebastian, and I head for Eastside Park. I'm not sure why I think so much more clearly in these circumstances. It's not that I'm at home in nature, such as it is. No one is going to confuse Eastside and Yellowstone Parks. But something about the quiet and tranquility, especially at night, helps me concentrate without exerting effort to do so.

The dogs also help. Life is simple to them: they want to smell the smells of the park, each time as if it's the first, yet they've been here so many times before. That simplicity makes sense, and it's something to enjoy and emulate, and maybe even envy.

Clear thinking doesn't always mean solutions, and we're halfway into the park and I haven't come up with anything. I am no closer to answering the core question than I was when I first took the case: Why was Kristen McNeil killed?

We're pretty far into the park and about to turn around when Tara tenses up and comes to a halt. I don't know what she has seen or sensed, but it has her on edge. Sebastian . . . not so much. He wouldn't react if John Philip Sousa appeared ahead of us, marching his band to Fair Lawn.

Then I see a glint of light come from behind a cluster of trees, and I go cold with panic. But the noise I hear is even stranger and more unexpected, a low, human voice. I think the word I hear is "Get."

Suddenly the noise changes and becomes much louder. It starts as a rustling in the grass, then explodes into what seems like a combination of growling and yelling, some human, some canine.

The latest noise seems to come from the area where I saw the glint of light. In the moonlight I can make out what is happening: a man is on the ground, being attacked by a dog.

None of this makes sense to me, and I look to see if the dog is Tara. But it obviously can't be because I am still holding on to both Tara's and Sebastian's leashes. Tara is excited and pulling on hers, seemingly trying to get in on whatever the action is. Sebastian seems bored with the whole thing.

Then I look to the side and see another human approaching the action. He leans over and picks something up, and I realize with some horror that he has picked up a gun. "Off," he says in a voice that's familiar to me, and the dog lets the guy go and backs off.

Finally it's all clear to me, even in this limited light. Corey Douglas and Simon have come to my rescue, even though I don't yet know who they have rescued me from.

Corey is holding his own gun; it could be the one he picked up, but I don't think so. "Turn around. Hands against the tree," he says to the man, who has just gotten to his feet.

The man does as he is told, but then whirls around, another gun having somehow appeared in his hand. But he doesn't get to use it because the deafening sound is Corey shooting him square in the chest. The impact of the bullet sends him backward, crashing into the tree, then he crumples to the ground.

Corey goes over to make sure the guy is

not getting up. "He's dead," he says, after feeling the guy's neck for whatever people in this situation feel necks for. Corey takes out his iPhone and activates the flashlight app, shining it in the dead guy's face. "You know who it is?"

I walk over and look. "I know who it is. Interpol has one less guy to find."

"Laurie told me to keep an eye on you," Corey says. "She said definitely not to tell you. She didn't say why, but I assumed it had something to do with you being an asshole."

"I'm glad you and Simon were here."

"I owe you. We owe you." I think he means he and Simon. "Remember?"

I nod. "Owed . . . past tense. We are way more than even now."

"Who is he? What did you mean about Interpol?"

"He's an international criminal, and a killer as well. The entire world is looking for this guy, and you nailed him."

Corey pats Simon's head. "We nailed him." Then, "I'll call in the department."

"I want to see what he has on him first."

"Hey." The cop in Corey thinks that I should not touch a thing.

"I'll replace it all exactly as I found it."

So using my own iPhone flashlight, I take everything out of Arrant's pockets. His wallet has nothing in it to identify him by his actual name; instead he has two different sets of fake identification. I memorize the names, put the wallet back, and keep looking.

There is probably $3,000 in cash, which I have no interest in. There is also a hotel key, one of the magnetic kinds that slide into the door. It is from the Marriott in Saddle Brook, maybe ten minutes from where we are standing . . . or in Arrant's case, not standing.

Corey is on the phone and doesn't seem to be looking, so I slip the key into my pocket. It doesn't make me feel great to deceive the guy who just saved my life, but I'll get over it. Simon is watching me but doesn't say anything, maybe out of friendship and respect for Tara.

Within five minutes Eastside Park is lit up like it's daytime. At least ten police cars with lights flashing and two ambulances are here. Once the EMTs certify that Arrant is dead, which will be rather easy to do, they'll call in the coroner's van. Then, when forensics is finished doing their work, he'll be carted off.

I call Laurie to tell her what happened,

and while she's upset, that feeling is obviously offset by my being safe and talking to her. "You had Corey on me without telling me."

"Guilty as charged."

We decide that Laurie will get a neighbor to come over and watch Ricky while she comes to the park to retrieve Tara and Sebastian. I'm going to be here for a long time, answering questions and signing statements. But bringing Ricky with her is not an option; as parents we try not to bring him to check out dead bodies.

I get off the phone when Pete pulls up and comes over to Corey and me. "That's Arrant?"

I nod. "That's him. Try not to let him escape."

Pete turns to Corey. "I assume you did the shooting? All Andy can do under pressure is piss in his pants."

Corey nods. "It was me. He drew a second weapon after Simon got him to drop the first one. Everything by the book."

Pete doesn't answer, but he doesn't have to. The scene speaks for itself; I was obviously walking the dogs in the park and Arrant was there to take me down. It didn't work out for him, thanks to Corey and Simon.

Tara did her part also, just less dramatically. Her tensing up at sensing Arrant's presence caused me to stop walking toward him, which may have been crucial. But it's just like Tara to let everyone else take the credit.

Finally Pete says, "Let's get this over with."

The "getting over with" part takes about three hours. We do it down at the precinct, so the interviews can be recorded. It's all straightforward and there will not be repercussions. It's made even easier for Pete that Corey is no longer on the force; "officer-involved" shootings are much more complicated.

This is going to be fairly clean for Pete and the Paterson Police. They will alert the Feds, and Arrant will instantly become their problem. If ballistics can help Pete nail Arrant for the murders of Taillon, Siroka and Holzer, then it will be a clean sweep.

We're done at around 1:00 A.M. and the cops drive us back to my house; Corey's car is parked just down the street. But Corey doesn't head for the car; instead he waits for me to go inside.

"You can go; I'm fine by myself."

"All evidence to the contrary. I do what Laurie tells me. I'm with you until you are in the house. Then she takes over."

"Are you going to kiss me good night?"

"Not a chance."

"Good. Corey . . . you saved my life. You and Simon. You both were amazing. So thank you."

"We did our job, just like you did when we were in court."

With that, I go into the house, and they turn and walk away. Laurie is waiting with some fresh coffee and a hug, not necessarily in that order. I go over the events of the night in slightly less detail than she would want because I'm tired. But I don't leave out anything crucial.

When I'm done, I take out the hotel key and show it to her.

"What's that?"

"A key to Arrant's hotel room."

"You took it off his body?"

I nod. "I did. I want to get a look in there."

"I would think that the police are all over it already."

"I don't think so. I'm sure he used one of two fake IDs, but by the time the cops make the connection and trace it to a hotel, we'll have been in and out of there."

"We?"

"I thought you might like to come along. Think of it as a morning adventure."

I call Sam and he answers on the first ring, in typical Sam fashion. "Talk to me." His voice sounds less raspy.

"You feeling better?"

"Getting there. What do you need?"

"Can you get into the computer at the Saddle Brook Marriott?"

"Why do you insult me? Of course."

"I need to know what room a particular guest is in."

"What's the name?"

I give him both names since I don't know which fake one Arrant used. I hope there's not a third name that I'm not aware of.

We get off the phone and Laurie and I head to bed. I'm exhausted; almost getting shot and killed can take a lot out of a person. I'm just falling asleep when the phone rings. Caller ID tells me that it's Sam.

"Hello?"

"Room 316, in the name of Edward Pruett. He was due to stay there another week."

We drop Ricky off at school and head for the hotel.

We want to get there early, when it will be busy, and there will be even less chance of our being noticed. Many people use the hotel for access to Manhattan, as well as Newark Airport, so the turnover of guests is rapid. Many of those people, I would assume, check out after breakfast.

Sam Willis meets us in the lobby; he's feeling better and wanted in on the action. I asked him to come in case we find any electronic devices that we need help on. He's going to wait downstairs and come up if I call him; we don't want to look like an invading army heading for Arrant's room.

We walk directly to the elevator and take it to the third floor. We smile and chat on the way, trying to appear normal, even though appearing normal is not necessarily my specialty. Once we get off the elevator, we follow the signs to room 316, which is at the end of the hall.

I insert the key and the light flashes green, always a good sign. Laurie goes in first; I opt not to carry her across the threshold.

"He had a suite," she says. "Crime pays."

She hands me a pair of skintight rubber gloves and puts a pair on herself. She seems a bit uncomfortable; this kind of subterfuge is not consistent with her cop's training. I doubt she's ever searched a room without getting a warrant.

We go through the entire room, which is not difficult or time-consuming because he traveled lightly. Just some clothes, and not much else, certainly not anything interesting. He also has two books on the night table, including a thriller by David Rosenfelt, who I hear is terrific. I'm tempted to grab it, but I don't.

A cell phone is in the night table drawer, so I call Sam and tell him to come up. He does, and Laurie hands him a pair of gloves. "This is so cool," he says.

He picks up the phone and examines it, pressing some buttons and looking like he knows what he's doing, which he does. He does so for two or three minutes.

"Got to be a burner phone," he says.

"Why?"

"There's no protection on it, no security."

"What does that mean?" I ask.

"Personal phones require a fingerprint, or facial ID, or at least a password. This has none of that; it's all there to be examined by anyone who wants to. I'd bet anything he was about to throw this one away. He must buy them by the truckload."

"What does he have on it?" Laurie asks.

"Not much; no emails, no downloads, no apps . . . none of that."

"What about phone calls?"

He nods. "He made three of them; doesn't seem to have received any."

"So you can tell who he called?" Laurie asks.

"For now all I know are what numbers he called, but I can definitely attach names to it. Won't take long. Are we taking the phone with us?"

"No," I say.

"Then give me a second to write down the numbers." Sam does just that. Then, "We leaving together?"

"No, you head out, and then Laurie and I will follow once we make sure everything is the way we found it."

Sam leaves and Laurie and I restore the few things we moved. As we leave, we wipe the outside doorknob clean. "I feel like a thief," she says.

"All for a good cause."

Once we're in the car, I call Pete. "What now?" he asks.

"I just got the weirdest anonymous tip. It said that Arrant was staying at the Saddle Brook Marriott in room 316 using the name Edward Pruett."

"An anonymous tip," he repeats, obviously skeptical.

"Yes. It was an anonymous tip left anonymously by a tipster who prefers to remain anonymous in order to retain his or her anonymity."

"The Feds were all over this early this morning. I'll relay this information."

"Do me a favor? Tell them you got it anonymously."

I hate jury selection.

Picking jurors, deciding which ones are most likely to buy the bullshit that we will be selling, is obviously crucial. For example, you would be hard-pressed to find a legal observer who doesn't believe that the O. J. Simpson case was lost in that pretrial phase.

What makes it so frustrating and detestable for me is that the reveal, the discovery of whether I made the right decisions, doesn't come until the end of the trial.

Then it's too late.

So I'm here for the second and hopefully last day of jury selection, trying my best and, more important, trying not to second-guess every decision I make.

Hike is not exactly helpful in these situations; he is sure that every potential juror would love nothing more than to send Noah to the electric chair, if New Jersey had one.

The only consolation is that the prosecutor, Jenna Silverman, has no clue either. She has a team of assistants and a jury specialist to consult with, which may or may not give her a sense of security, but it would be false. Like me, she'll have to wait until the end to find out if she made the right calls.

We should be done by lunchtime, and Judge Calvin Stiller has said we would start with opening statements tomorrow.

This shouldn't be a long trial, but it will take quite a while to play out. That's because we are starting on Monday, but then we'll stop for Christmas on Friday, then stop again for New Year's Day. I only wish that instead of viewing Christmas as a short-duration event, the court would adopt Laurie's three-month Christmas window. By then we might be ready to mount a decent defense.

Both Jenna and I urged Judge Stiller to wait until after New Year's to start. He didn't listen to us for two reasons. First, he considers any day that isn't utilized to be a crime against nature. Second, anything a lawyer recommends is something he instinctively resists. Maybe I should recommend Noah's conviction.

Judge Stiller does not like me. That is not breaking news; if I was going to practice in a courtroom where the judge didn't dislike me, it would have to be on the moon. The only factor in my favor is that he dislikes all lawyers, which sort of evens the playing field.

Sam calls me during lunch with some news that seems bizarre. He's traced the three phone calls on Arrant's burner phone. One was to Taillon, which makes perfect sense. He might even have been calling him to arrange the Pennington Park meeting that resulted in Taillon's and Siroka's deaths.

The second call was to Gameday, a video-game company in Oklahoma. I have no idea why that call was made, and since it went through the company switchboard, there's no way to know who received it. The call could have been benign, though Arrant's profile doesn't seem to be that of video-game nerd.

The third call is even weirder. He called an assistant football coach at LSU named Ben Walther, who is the defensive co-ordinator. Walther has developed a national reputation and is said to be a leading candidate for some head-coaching jobs after the season.

The call lasted ten minutes. LSU is playing Clemson in a national semifinal game in a couple of weeks, so Walther must be pretty damn busy. But he found time to take Arrant's call.

If I had to guess, based on Arrant's criminal history and ability to profit off of it, I would say that some illegal betting or fixing is going on. But that's a stretch; this is big-time college football with great scrutiny on it. Also, I am not aware of anything in Arrant's past that involved sports betting.

It could also be some kind of recruiting scandal, but for it to be lucrative enough to attract someone like Arrant, it would have to be widespread. With only the one call to the one coach, at least on this phone, it seems even more unlikely.

I assume that the Feds have already been to the Marriott and retrieved Arrant's phone. By now they should know who he called and will no doubt follow up on it. But I can't count on them to do anything on my time schedule, nor will they share with me what they learn.

If Arrant had any information on who is going to win the LSU-Clemson game, I wish he had shared it with me before he died. I bet on bowl games all the time, and I think the last one I won involved players wearing leather helmets.

Unfortunately, I believe that Arrant died

with the answer to all my questions. The key one is how an international criminal like Arrant became involved in the murder of eighteen-year-old Kristen McNeil.

Is it so simple that he had a client who was, for whatever reason, willing to pay to have her killed? Was he just a hired killer who farmed the job out to Taillon to literally execute? Or was there more to it? Did Kristen somehow represent a threat to Arrant or the people that paid him? I haven't found anything that would indicate this and I'm running out of time.

But there's no opportunity to think about it now; I have a fun afternoon of guessing what a bunch of people who have no desire to serve on a jury will do once they get stuck on one.

Juror candidate number 37 is staring at Noah; does that mean she hates him or is sympathetic to him? Or is she staring at Hike, who is sitting next to Noah? I'm going to accept her to sit on this trial, and if she votes to convict, I'm going to somehow set her up on a blind date with Hike.

Revenge will be mine.

The jury has finally been chosen and it's terrific, or awful.

We'll know when we know. One thing is certain. It is what it is, they are who they are, and there's no upside in my focusing on it or worrying about it. Time to move on.

So with the afternoon free before opening statements tomorrow, I go home and do what I do almost every day, starting well before the trial and continuing until the jury starts deliberating. I read through the discovery documents.

I do this even though I almost know them by heart already. It's partially because I need to be ultraprepared for anything that comes up during the trial; I need to be able to react quickly and by instinct, rather than strain to remember something I read.

The other reason is that on many occasions reading something, even dry evidentiary reports, somehow causes me to look at an issue with fresh eyes, and I see something I hadn't seen before.

After about an hour, fresh eyes and new discoveries are nowhere to be found, so my mind starts to wander. These pages are all about the evidence against Noah. They obviously have nothing to do with the case I am trying to develop, albeit unsuccessfully.

The prosecution will never admit that four dead bodies now connect to this case, those of Taillon, Siroka, Holzer, and Arrant. I would have replaced Arrant as one of the four in the group if not for the intervention of Corey Douglas and the amazing Simon.

I certainly believe that Arrant killed Taillon, Siroka, and Holzer and was set on killing me. But I have to say that it seems like literal "overkill"; Arrant reacted violently and lethally to situations that just did not seem that threatening to him. But he obviously thought otherwise.

Taillon and Siroka worked for Arrant and might therefore have been privy to information that could have endangered him. Therefore, killing them could have made some sense.

But why Holzer and me? All Holzer had was Arrant's name and a suspicion. He didn't know where Arrant was and certainly could not prove that he was involved in anything. I still don't know how Arrant even knew that Holzer had his name, unless Arrant has connections to the Paterson streets. It's hard to see why he would.

Arrant killed Holzer and went after me soon after Holzer and I talked. What made him move so swiftly? And why go after me? How would Arrant even know that Holzer told me Arrant's name?

I can't imagine we have a leak in our organization; we barely have an organization. And it's highly unlikely we have electronic surveillance on us. Holzer was killed the day after talking to me; there's no way taps and microphones could have been placed, and the information derived acted upon, so quickly.

I keep bouncing around back and forth between things I don't understand, so in keeping with that, I once again focus on Kristen McNeil. Why was she killed?

The only people that come close to being suspects in my mind are the Wainwrights, father Arthur and son Kyle. Each brings his own issues to the suspect party. Kyle was Kristen's boyfriend, and she was dumping and cheating on him. Anger at rejection therefore becomes a possible motive.

Arthur Wainwright, as the father of Kyle,

could also be involved. But what makes him intriguing is his wealth. Arrant did not come cheap, and he then turned around and hired Taillon, who hired Siroka. Taillon had $20,000 in his possession, very possibly his payment for having me followed, and who knows what else.

But money seems to be all over their actions and this case, and Arthur Wainwright has plenty of it.

One thing I have not focused on is Net-Link Systems itself. It is a successful company and Kristen worked there. She could have met someone else there who has some direct or indirect involvement in this case. That's at least a better bet than the answer being among her high school friends. Net-Link could be described as Kristen's connection to the real world, and a high-stakes world at that.

Even more significant, we know that Taillon called NetLink twice just before Kristen was killed. I still don't know who he called — it could even have been Kristen herself — but the connection between Taillon and someone at NetLink is crucial.

I take out Sam's reports on Taillon's phone calls, but nothing more is to be learned there. I need to be aggressive and try to shake things up, so I decide to call

Jeremy Kennon, the tech guy that Kyle works for. At least he didn't throw me out of his office, which is more than I can say for Arthur Wainwright.

The phone number for NetLink is right here in Sam's report of Taillon's phone calls. Assuming it's still the number, I dial it. It rings twice, and a woman answers, "Mr. Wainwright's office. How may I help you?"

I'm surprised by this; I thought I'd be reaching the switchboard. It sounds like I'm talking to the woman who brought me to Arthur Wainwright's office when I was there. "Hello, this is Andy Carpenter. We met last week, and —"

"Hello, Mr. Carpenter. How can I help you?"

"I was trying to reach Jeremy Kennon."

"Oh, let me switch you to the operator. This is Mr. Wainwright's private line."

"No thank you. I've got another call coming in, so I'll call back," I lie.

When we get off the call, I let the impact of what I've just learned sink in. Taillon didn't just call NetLink Systems twice the week of Kristen McNeil's murder.

He called Arthur Wainwright.

"I have been through too many trials to minimize the importance of your job."

That's how Jenna Silverman begins her opening statement. With the first sentence, I can tell she is going to be a problem for the good guys, in this case us.

First of all, she looks the part. She's attractive but buttoned-down and professional, seeming to be serious and in control. She speaks in a pleasant but authoritative voice. She is someone you want to root for, whose side you want to be on.

She continues, "There really are very few tasks that you will do in your life, that anyone will do in their life, that are more significant. You will go in a room, no lawyers or judges will be around, and you will decide the fate of another human being. Your decision will either send him to prison for most of the rest of his life, or free him, never to be bothered by these charges again.

"But I have also been part of enough trials to know that there is a difference between important and difficult. I'm going to be blunt here: your job is not difficult.

"Very often there are complicated issues involved in a trial, sometimes requiring a special expertise. This is not one of those cases. We will demonstrate through forensic evidence that cannot be challenged that Noah Traynor was with Kristen McNeil at the time and place of her death. That same evidence will prove that they had a violent confrontation.

"When I say that these facts cannot be challenged, I will predict that Mr. Carpenter will not even make the attempt. That's how irrefutable that evidence is.

"But Mr. Carpenter is an excellent attorney, and he is nothing if not resourceful. So he will parade a group of criminals before you, some dead and some alive. The one thing they will all have in common is that they are not relevant to this case, so you should not let them distract you from the facts.

"We will also show a consciousness of guilt that caused Mr. Traynor to avoid acknowledging these facts for fourteen years. If there was an innocent explanation, why not come forward with it? Why not do what you can to help the police find this awful killer, who could conceivably strike again? Why hide in the shadows for all this time?

"The answer will be crystal clear and not difficult for you to uncover. That answer is that Noah Traynor willfully and cold-bloodedly strangled eighteen-year-old Kristen McNeil and left her body lying in the dirt.

"Maybe, after fourteen years, he felt secure that he would not be discovered, that the secret died with Kristen. But the truth is out, and after so long, Kristen will finally have her justice.

"Thank you for listening and thank you for serving."

Judge Stiller gives me the floor, and I stand to give our opening statement. "Ladies and gentlemen, Ms. Silverman is correct in some of what she told you. She will present evidence saying that Kristen McNeil and Noah Traynor were together at the murder scene and that they had a disagreement that turned physical.

"We will not dispute any of that; we will acknowledge it and accept it as fact. We encourage you to do the same. But she will go on to say that those facts mean that Noah Traynor murdered Kristen McNeil, and we will vigorously dispute that, because they don't, and he didn't.

"Ms. Silverman describes Mr. Traynor's failure to come forward and tell his story as consciousness of guilt. It is not; it is consciousness of fear. The media was going crazy back then; they were buying the police theory that whoever left the DNA evidence behind was the guilty party.

"Mr. Traynor knew that if he was found to be the person with that DNA, he would be accused of the murder, no matter what he said. The fact that we are here today is evidence that he was right. Perhaps he should have come forward anyway, but his not doing so was out of fear, not guilt.

"But keep one thing in mind. While Ms. Silverman would have you believe that an innocent Mr. Traynor would have come forward to help the police find the real killer, that simply is not true. He had no more idea who the real killer was than the police did.

"This tragic murder did not happen in a vacuum and was not the result of a dispute among teenagers. Kristen McNeil was caught in a world that she could not handle, with evil people who cared nothing about her life. So they took her life and went on with theirs.

"You will meet those people, though some of them are no longer with us, additional victims of the violent world in which they lived. Noah Traynor has never been part of that world, and never will be.

"Thank you."

Jeremy Kennon has agreed to meet me here, at my office.

He is doing so despite an obvious reluctance to meet with me at all. That he's come here is, I suspect, because he doesn't want to be seen with me at his office, or in a public place.

It hurts my feelings, but I'll get over it.

Kennon shows up at ten after six, which is only ten minutes late. He was coming from his office, so maybe work got in the way. In any event, he makes no effort to apologize.

"Thanks for coming."

"No problem. Nice place you got here, right above the fruit market. Do you pick up a cantaloupe when you drop off the rent check?"

"How did you know that? Get one when you leave, and get some peaches as well; they're unlike anything you've ever tasted."

He nods; I don't think he wants to continue a fruit-based conversation. "Anyway, better we meet here than at my office; you're not that well loved at NetLink right now."

"I'm really a joy, once you get to know me."

He grins. "I'll bet. But if you're waiting for an invite to the NetLink Christmas party, you can safely make other plans."

"I'll do that."

"So why am I here?"

"I need you to give me a road map. I think that Kristen McNeil may have been having a relationship with someone at NetLink."

He nods. "Kyle Wainwright. We've been over that."

"I'm talking about someone older."

"Can you be more specific?"

I shake my head. "I wish I could. That's why I need you to give me a road map, tell me who she had contact with while she was there. It doesn't have to be someone who is a current employee."

He pauses for a while. "I'd have to think about it. It's been a lot of years, and she wasn't in my department."

"She worked for Arthur Wainwright, didn't she?"

He nods. "As an intern-slash-assistant."

"Anything unusual about their relationship?"

"Oh, come on. You can't possibly think that Arthur would . . ."

"I don't know Arthur. My only contact with him was when he threw me out of his office, and I thought he handled that with incredible charm and grace."

"He was being protective of his son."

"His son is not eighteen anymore, and why would he need protection in the first place?"

Kennon, instead of answering the question, says, "I owe everything to Arthur Wainwright. He's believed in me, he's mentored me, he's promoted me, he's paid me. You will not get me to say anything bad about him because I have nothing bad to say about him."

"I'm not trying to. What I'm trying to do is get a picture of what Kristen McNeil's work life was like fourteen years ago."

He nods. "I'll think about that, but I doubt I'll come up with much. I don't think your answer is at NetLink, but I know it is not in Arthur Wainwright's office."

I'm not going to push it with Kennon; he's clearly not going to give me any negative information on Wainwright, and I don't want Kennon warning Wainwright that he's on my radar. But he is dead center on it.

Taillon called Arthur Wainwright. That is a crucial piece of information, and while I'm not sharing it with Kennon, I'm going to share it with the jury.

What I need to focus on now is what Wainwright's motive could have been. I can come up with a number of possibilities, but what they all have in common is that they don't stand up to logical scrutiny.

The most obvious, but least likely, is that Arthur was exacting revenge on behalf of his son. Kristen was dumping Kyle, and likely cheating on him, so Arthur had her killed. That would seem like a ridiculous overreaction, and I can't see Arthur going there.

Another possibility is that Arthur was the older man Kristen spoke about. Maybe she was pressuring him, and he was afraid of the devastation to his life and reputation of the revelation that he was having an affair with a teenage girl. So he killed her to keep her quiet, as a means of self-protection.

A third theory might be that she had learned something about Arthur's business life that would have been devastating to him and maybe NetLink should it have been made public. This is somewhat more likely than the two previous theories, but that's only because it's a low bar to get over. Net-Link has operated without a hint of scandal for the past fourteen years, which argues against its harboring an awful secret.

The only thing I know for sure is that Taillon was in touch with Arthur Wainwright around the time of Kristen McNeil's murder.

If Noah Traynor is going to get his freedom back, I'm going to have to figure out why.

Sergeant Theresa Swanson is Jenna's first witness.

She is here simply to set the scene, in this case the crime scene. Swanson and her partner, Luther Jackson, were the first officers there. Swanson was just a patrolwoman at the time; Jackson has since retired from the force.

"What brought you to Hinchliffe Stadium that day?" Jenna asks.

"There was a nine-one-one call reporting a body that was found there. A teenager named Douglas McCann had seen the body, ran home, and told his father, who called nine-one-one."

"Were they there when you arrived?"

Swanson nods. "They were."

"Please describe what you saw."

"A young female adult was lying in the shrubbery. She was wearing a blue blouse and a pair of jeans. The blouse was torn, and the jeans were unbuttoned but not pulled down and not torn. We determined that she was deceased. There were no obvious wounds, but her head and neck were bent at an unnatural angle."

"What did you do?"

"We called in the report, as well as bringing in EMS and the coroner, and secured the scene."

"Did you see any signs of a possible perpetrator?" Jenna asks.

"We did not."

"How long was it before backup arrived?"

"Homicide detectives were there within seven minutes, and we turned the scene over to them. The ambulance and forensics both arrived a few minutes after that."

"Did you examine Ms. McNeil's body?"

"We did not, other than to determine that she was deceased and could not be helped by CPR."

Jenna has photographs of the scene and body projected onto the screen set up in the courtroom. The jury seems to recoil in horror when they see Kristen's body, as Jenna knew they would. That is why she had the photos shown; they don't say anything that hadn't already been described.

But the tactic is powerful, and even though the pictures are not at all gory, they are devastating images. A young girl was lying in the dust and shrubs, her life and dignity taken from her. The jury is going to want to punish someone for that, and their only option is Noah.

I can get nothing from Swanson on cross-examination, so I decline to ask any questions. I don't want to appear to be nitpicking since I have already said in opening statements that we are not going to claim that Noah was not there.

Swanson said nothing negative about Noah at all, which will make her unique among the prosecution witnesses. But with only a limited number of bullets in my cross-examination gun, I'll save them for when they might be able to do damage.

The next witness Jenna calls is Lieutenant Stan Oglesby, of the Homicide Division. He is a direct report to Pete Stanton, who has often told me that Oglesby is an outstanding cop. Pete said that as if it was a positive; if he was a defense attorney, he might feel differently.

Oglesby arrived at the scene and took control of it, but the visual he describes is similar to how Swanson described it.

"Were you able to determine the time of death?" Jenna asks.

"I didn't try; that is much better left to

the coroner. But there were certain signs that she had been there for some length of time." Jenna does not have him describe those signs, much to the relief of the jury and probably everyone else in the courtroom.

"Were you able to identify the body?"

He nods. "She still had her wallet in her possession, with her driver's license and credit cards in it. Also, her car was in the parking lot, and it contained her registration and insurance card."

"Any cash?"

"Twelve bucks."

"What did the fact that her car was there tell you?"

"Again, I was just gathering information at that point, but it was and is pretty clear that her killer had his own means of transportation."

When I get to question Oglesby, I say, "I'm going to ask you some questions. Please either answer them, or if you can't, just say, 'I don't know.' "

Jenna objects that I'm improperly instructing the witness, and Judge Stiller sustains. My first question for Oglesby is "Let's start with your last comment about transportation. You said the killer had his own means of transportation. What type of transportation was it?"

"What do you mean?"

"Was it a car? A bicycle? Did he take a bus and walk to the stadium?"

"I can't say."

"Why can't you say?"

"Because I don't know the answer."

I nod. "Okay. Were the killer and Ms. Mc-Neil the only two people present?"

"I can't say for sure."

"You don't know?" I ask.

"Correct."

"As to the exact place where you found the body, is that where she was killed?"

"I saw no evidence otherwise."

"So you're certain of it?"

"Not certain, no."

"Why was Kristen McNeil at Hinchliffe Stadium?"

"You want me to speculate?"

"No. If you're sure, then please tell us. If you don't know, that's fine too. I'm only interested in facts."

"I can't be sure."

"Okay," I say. "Now that we know what you don't know, let's move on to what you do know. I know we are going to hear from the medical examiner later, but if you know, what was the cause of death?"

"Strangulation."

"Was her neck broken?"

"Yes."

"If you were to grab someone from behind and choke them, would their neck necessarily break in that fashion?"

"Not necessarily."

"Would there have to be a violent twisting, rather than just a choking?"

"Probably."

"Sort of the way it is taught in hand-to-hand combat in the military?"

"I couldn't say."

I nod. "Okay. For most of the fourteen years since the murder, was Noah Traynor on a suspect list?"

"No."

"You never questioned him?"

"No."

"Had you ever even heard the name Noah Traynor before the DNA match came through?"

"No, I don't believe so."

"Did you interview many of Kristen's friends?" I ask.

"Yes."

"None of them mentioned him?"

"No."

"Once he became a suspect, did you check him out fully? Look into his past?"

"Of course."

"Did he have any convictions before the day Kristen McNeil was killed?"

"No."

"Any arrests, before or since?"

"No."

"Speeding tickets? Illegal parking?"

"No."

"Littering? Swearing in public?"

Jenna stands and objects, but before she can get it out, Oglesby has already answered, "No."

"Lieutenant, in your experience, is it unusual for a person to commit a vicious, almost professional-style, cold-blooded murder and yet live the entire rest of his life without doing anything wrong?"

"Every case is different."

I frown. "Thank you for sharing that. No further questions."

The conversation with Carpenter left Kennon more than a little unsure about what to do.

Carpenter seemed to be coming after Net-Link Systems in general, and Arthur Wainwright in particular; Carpenter as much as said so. Kennon wasn't sure how to react, or if he needed to react at all.

Finally, he decided to talk about it with Kyle Wainwright. Not wanting to do so in the office, they met for a drink at a small bar in Englewood, not far from where Kyle lived.

They ordered drinks and Kyle said, "Don't keep me in suspense; what did you want to talk about?"

"Andy Carpenter."

"Has he been around again?"

Kennon nodded. "I talked to him out of the office. He's asking a bunch of questions about people that Kristen was friendly with at NetLink."

"How would you know who she was friendly with?"

"I wouldn't, and that's what I told him. But the reason we're here is that he's asking questions specifically about your father. I think he has the idea that he might have been having an affair with Kristen."

Kyle laughed. "Oh, come on . . . seriously?"

"He didn't come out and say it, but that's the impression I got."

"My father barely even touched my mother. Maybe once, and they had me. My father figured that was plenty."

"You're missing the point, Kyle. If he thinks that Arthur was having an affair with Kristen, it's a short jump to thinking he killed her to cover it up. All Carpenter is interested in is blaming someone else for the murder."

"Let him try."

"You're not thinking about the company. If Carpenter winds up accusing Arthur in open court, it could spook our clients. Once a charge like that is out there, it never completely goes away, no matter what. Doesn't matter if it's true or not."

"Shit."

"And sometimes it never gets erased,"

Kennon said.

"You're not saying you think it could be true, are you?"

Kennon shook his head. "That's not the Arthur I know, not even close, but people do crazy things. It could have been an accident, but . . . no, at the end of the day I don't think it could be true."

"You think I should tell him what Carpenter is doing?"

"It might help him deal with this; maybe he'd hire a lawyer to keep Carpenter off his ass."

"Why don't you tell him?"

Kennon laughed at the idea. "No chance. In a lot of ways Arthur has been like a father to me, but he's not actually my father. That honor falls to you."

"I'll think about it. But that is not a conversation I would look forward to. He'd go absolutely batshit crazy."

Kennon laughed again and stood up. "My work here is done." Then, "Seriously, I may be reading too much into this, but I thought you should know. I don't think your father is in any jeopardy, but if Carpenter makes public noises, it could be aggravating for him. That's all."

Kyle nodded. "I hear you."

I'm of two minds about Janet Carlson.

Outside the courtroom she is a pleasure . . . smart, funny, and compassionate. She is also, without a doubt, the best-looking coroner on the planet.

That's not a particularly high bar; most coroners that I've met aren't what you would consider lookers. Few beauty-pageant contestants say, "I want to create world peace, eliminate hunger, and cut up as many dead bodies as I can get my hands on."

But inside the courtroom, and particularly on the witness stand, I'm not a big fan of hers. By definition she always testifies for the prosecution, which makes her my enemy. Her intelligence, coupled with her calm and unruffled demeanor, make her someone I don't look forward to questioning.

Jenna has no such reservations. She starts by asking if Janet did the autopsy on Kristen McNeil.

"No, that was done by Dr. Paul Griffith; he was my predecessor."

"Dr. Griffith has since passed away, is that correct?"

Janet nods. "Yes. Six years ago."

Janet says that she has studied the autopsy results, and that she is prepared to discuss them. "Dr. Griffith was very meticulous in his work."

Under questioning, Janet says that Kristen died of asphyxiation as the result of strangulation. Janet repeats earlier testimony that her neck was broken, and her larynx crushed, but the lack of air was the immediate cause of death.

"So this was done powerfully?"

Janet nods. "Yes. Very much so."

"In your professional opinion, could it have been done accidentally, perhaps during rough sex?"

"No, I would say not, and Dr. Griffith specifically discounted that possibility. In addition to the nature of the strangulation, there was no evidence of sexual activity."

"Were there any other signs of a struggle?"

Janet nods. "Her blouse was torn, and she had skin tissue under her fingernails."

Jenna goes over the rest of the autopsy with Janet, but there is nothing of any great significance. Kristen had no drugs or alcohol in her system, which I suppose Jenna brings out to further demonstrate her purity and innocence. It's unnecessary; that she was brutally strangled and left in the dirt is tragic regardless of any other personal facts.

The photographs come out again, just in case the jury has forgotten what the body and the scene looked like.

Once again I have no ammunition to attack the prosecution witness; everything they are saying is borne out by the evidence. They are not presenting theories, they are presenting facts.

"Just to reconfirm what you said," I begin, "Kristen McNeil's blouse was torn, her jeans were unbuttoned, but there was no evidence of sexual activity, forced or otherwise?"

"Correct."

"Does that seem strange to you?"

"That is not within my purview."

"What about outside your purview? Does it seem strange there?"

"Somewhat."

"Let's talk about the skin fragments found under Kristen McNeil's fingernails. Did Dr. Griffith estimate when they arrived there?"

"What do you mean?"

"Well, he estimated a time of death within

a four-hour window. Did he say when she got the skin fragments under her fingernails, in relation to the time of death?"

Janet shakes her head. "No."

"Could it have been moments before death?"

"Certainly."

"How about ten minutes before?"

A slight shrug. "It's possible."

"An hour before? Two hours?"

"Dr. Griffith would have had no way of knowing that."

"When she got the skin under her nails, where was she?"

"Meaning . . . ?" Janet prompts.

"Meaning was it even at Hinchliffe Stadium? Could she have been somewhere else entirely?"

"Again, no way of knowing."

"So it's possible?"

Janet nods. "Yes."

"Can you say with certainty that the person whose skin was under her nails was the killer?"

"I cannot."

"Thank you. No further questions."

Judge Stiller has done us a favor.

Jenna had set it up so that her final witness was going to testify just prior to Christmas, and then the last thing the jury would hear would be her resting the prosecution's case. That witness is going to be presenting the forensics, which is the devastating part of the case.

The jurors would thus spend the holiday having heard from one side only. The prosecution would have that tremendous advantage, and jurors would be leaning toward believing Noah to be guilty. Those views would have time to harden and set over the holiday.

But I think that Stiller saw that coming and considered it an unfair advantage. He therefore had us adjourn for the holiday a day early. He wouldn't admit the real meaning, so instead he unconvincingly mumbled something about his belief that the holiday starts a day early, on Christmas Eve.

Christmas Day at our house is traditionally a re-creation of the Thanksgiving Day experience, the only notable difference being that I watch NBA basketball instead of NFL football. For years now the NBA has co-opted the day, forcing their top teams to play rather than stay home with their families.

Once again Laurie has invited Julie and Danny Traynor, and once again they have brought Murphy. The mood is more subdued than it was over Thanksgiving. Back then the trial hadn't started, so there was optimism that all would go well.

Julie has been in court every day, and it has not been fun for her. She can tell where this is going, as can pretty much everyone else, including the jurors. It hasn't been a barrel of laughs for me either. In any event, we do not discuss the trial whatsoever.

But Laurie has made sure that there are tons of presents to go around. I'm pretty tough to buy for; I don't need or want anything that I don't already have. But Laurie has gotten me a pair of great seats to an upcoming Eagles concert. I like the Eagles, but she absolutely loves them, so she's thrilled with the gift. She assumes I am going to take her, rather than get another date.

Once the Traynor contingent has left, I head for my walking/thinking trek with Tara and Sebastian. I haven't been through the park since the night Arrant came after me. I don't know if Laurie still has Corey and Simon watching for me; I hope not. But walking on the streets seems safer than the park, just in case.

Thinking back on that night, I still don't know why Arrant felt it necessary to come after Holzer and me in rapid succession. It's been bugging me ever since then how Arrant even knew that Holzer had given me his name.

The only person who knew about it, other than Laurie, Marcus, and me, was Holzer's "idiot goon." He was on the ground but awake when Holzer said it, but he should have had absolutely no reason to be connected to Arrant.

I wish I knew the significance of Arrant's death. He could have been just one layer in a chain that went up from Siroka to Taillon to Arrant, with others above him. Or he could have been at the top of that chain.

I'm leaning toward the former theory. Taillon's phone calls to Arthur Wainwright around the time of the McNeil murder trump everything. It proves that Wainwright was involved.

Arrant worked for money, and Wainwright has plenty of it, so it makes sense that Arrant was a literal hired gun. But has he been replaced? If so, the replacement hasn't made his presence known yet, at least to me. But that doesn't mean he's not there, or that he won't suddenly become active.

But the question of whether he has been replaced, as does every other question in this case, depends on why Kristen McNeil was killed. If Arthur Wainwright was exacting revenge for his son or was himself having an affair with Kristen and wanted to cover it up, then a person in Arrant's role is not necessary.

But I am becoming less and less convinced that those theories are credible. If Kristen's death was for a reason as simple as that, then Wainwright would have had no logical reason to order the deaths of Taillon, Siroka, and Holzer. He's gotten away with it for fourteen years; why not just let the system run its course and convict Noah?

And even if Noah was somehow acquitted, or the jury was hung, so what? The police are not suddenly going to dive into a fourteen-year-old murder case and shine a light on Arthur Wainwright.

Far more likely is that Kristen McNeil had either been a part of, or a danger to, some ongoing conspiracy that Wainwright is desperate to keep operating and concealed. Then the scrutiny of a trial, and a lawyer like me investigating, would represent a problem worth killing to solve.

If love or sex or family was the motive for the murder, we have what is probably an insurmountable mountain to climb. I can cast suspicion on Arthur Wainwright, and I will, but I'll never be able to prove the facts.

If, on the other hand, there is an ongoing conspiracy, then somehow I need to uncover its existence and its perpetrators. That is the kind of case we will have to build for this jury for us to have a real chance.

So midway through the trial, I am clear on a strategy. Executing it? That's another story.

Cynthia and Kevin McNeil had not attended a single day of the trial.

They knew they would not be able to stand it; witnessing it would be far too painful. To watch their daughter spoken about as an object, to have to look away knowing that photographs of her lifeless and brutalized body were being shown to all of these strangers, that would be far too much.

And to be in the same room as the person who caused them all of their agony, well, that would simply be inconceivable. Their other daughter, Karen, felt differently. She felt that she had to see it, had to watch every moment of her sister's killer being brought to justice after all these years.

Karen kept them up-to-date, albeit delicately, and in her recounting, Noah Traynor was unquestionably the person who had taken their daughter from them. It reconfirmed in their minds the correctness of their decision not to speak to his lawyer, even though Karen said that the lawyer seemed to be decent and fair-minded. She said he was just doing his job, but the Mc-Neils saw no reason to help him do it.

A guilty verdict wouldn't bring what everyone called closure; that seemed like such a ridiculous concept that Cynthia and Kevin couldn't even wrap their minds around it. They thought that people who talked about closure must never have had anything to close. Losing Kristen would always be the dominant event in their lives, and nothing that could happen in any courtroom could change that.

But even though they didn't speak about it to each other, they both knew that it was time to stop running in place, to finally try to live as Kristen would have wanted them to.

They would somehow manage to do that as best they could, timed to the start of the new year.

I wish I could have called in sick today.

Jenna's powerful case can be summed up in one witness, and that's the one we're going to hear from in a little while. The jury seems to be sitting up a bit straighter in their chairs, which indicates to me that they know what's coming.

That further indicates that they are ignoring Judge Stiller's admonition not to read or watch anything about the trial in the media. Because the media has been quite clear that today is forensics day.

Jenna is going to heighten the anticipation by making everyone wait a bit longer. She calls as her first witness Arnie Pafko, who was a friend of Noah's back in the day.

Jenna establishes their relationship as high school buddies and fraternity brothers. She further gets him to say that they haven't seen or talked to each other in years, since she would know that I would bring that out on cross-examination. Then she gets down to the meat of it.

"Mr. Pafko, was there any time during which you were aware that Mr. Traynor knew Kristen McNeil?"

"Yes, he told me they were dating."

"How long before her death was this?"

He takes a moment to think, as if he is pondering the question for the first time. That is total bullshit since he and Jenna would have gone over this in advance a number of times. Finally he says, "Maybe a couple of weeks. I had gone away to college, so I wasn't aware of the murder until a few weeks after it happened."

"What else did he tell you besides the fact that he and Kristen were dating?"

He hesitates. "They were going to have sex. He was sure of it."

"What was your response?"

He grins. "I told him he was crazy. We didn't get lucky too often back in those days."

"And when you told him that? What did he say?"

"That he guaranteed it. He was bragging, which wasn't so unusual. But then he said, 'Believe me, she wants to.' So I said, 'She'll change her mind.' Then he said something which bothered me, and I won't forget it."

"What was that?"

"He said, 'Not if she knows what's good for her.'"

Jenna ends her examination on this dramatic note, which is a mistake, because I'm about to beat this witness to death with questions that she should have asked in a way that limited their impact.

"Mr. Pafko, why did the police ignore you when you told them you were concerned for Kristen McNeil's safety?"

"I didn't go to the police."

I feign surprise. "So you only told her parents?"

"I didn't tell them either. I didn't tell anybody."

"Why not?"

"I guess because I didn't really think Noah would do anything to hurt her. We did a lot of talking in those days, but not too much following through."

"I'm confused. You thought he would hurt her, or you didn't?"

"I guess I didn't, but looking back now, I should have taken action."

"Because she was killed," I say.

"Right."

"I can see that. Who at the Paterson Police Department did you talk to once you found out she was killed? And what did they say to you?"

"I didn't go to them. I should have."

"You just said that looking back, once she was killed, you should have taken action. But you actually didn't take action once you found out about it?"

"No; I feel guilty about that."

"This is the kind of guilt that doesn't kick in until fourteen years after the event? It's a slow-developing guilt?"

Jenna objects that I'm badgering him, but Judge Stiller overrules her and instructs him to answer.

"I'm not proud of my actions."

I nod. "That's the first thing you've said today that's believable."

Jenna jumps out of her seat to object, and before she even gets the words out, Judge Stiller sustains the objection, strikes my comment from the record, and instructs the jury to disregard it.

Good luck with that.

Jenna is pissed, which doesn't bother me in the least. Then she calls her last witness, which bothers me plenty.

Sergeant Xavier Jennings is two weeks away from retirement.

That is just one of many reasons I wish this trial was delayed. As a witness, Jennings is a major pain in the ass to defense attorneys.

Jennings has been in charge of forensics for the Paterson Police Department since about an hour after forensics was invented. He's seen everything, and not a defense attorney in New Jersey, yours truly included, can rattle or intimidate him.

He's also funny and self-effacing and smart. Outside the courtroom I like him; inside the courtroom I wish that he would spend an entire day stuck in an elevator with Hike.

As for juries . . . they eat him up with a spoon.

Hike is not here today; he is off making sure that we have scientific support for what our first witness is going to say tomorrow. We'd better have it, or we're dead in the water.

After Jenna establishes Jennings's credentials and position in the department, she asks, "Sergeant Jennings, were you in charge of forensics fourteen years ago, when Kristen McNeil was murdered?"

He smiles. "Yes. My career hasn't exactly taken off."

She returns the smile; they're having a blast. "Did you uncover any significant human DNA in the immediate area besides that of the victim?"

"Yes. We found DNA on a discarded beer can, on a chewed piece of gum, and most significantly, there were pieces of skin under the fingernails of the deceased."

"Did this DNA all belong to the same person?"

"Yes, it did."

"If that person is in the courtroom today, can you point him out?"

Jennings points to Noah, and Jenna confirms the identification. She asks a few more questions, bringing out that traces of Noah's blood were under the fingernails as well.

She then takes Jennings through the way the police got to Noah, describing the website that facilitated it. It's not important, but Jenna seems to want to keep Jennings on the stand as long as she can. This is the crux of her case, and she just wants to prolong it.

Finally I get to ask my questions, none of which are going to make a dent in Jennings's testimony. "Sergeant, this crime took place fourteen years ago, and you have had this DNA evidence all that time. Why did it take until now to identify who it belonged to?"

"The defendant's DNA was not included in any of the databases that we have access to."

"Are there any databases you don't have access to?"

"No."

"Had Mr. Traynor been arrested or convicted of a crime, either before or after the murder, his DNA would have been in one of these databases?"

"Yes."

"Sergeant, your work in this case demonstrates that Mr. Traynor was at some point at the scene of the crime, and that Ms. McNeil scratched Mr. Traynor in some fashion, is that correct?"

"Yes."

"Does it prove that he was on the scene when she was killed?"

"No."

"Does it prove that he committed the murder?"

"No."

"Thank you. No further questions."

Judge Stiller asks, "Ms. Silverman, do you have more witnesses to call?"

She stands. "No, Your Honor. The prosecution rests."

Judge Stiller adjourns for the day, telling me to be prepared to call our first witness in the morning.

I can see Noah is stunned by today's testimony; he knew it was coming, but to expect it is very different from actually experiencing it. If he's honest with himself, then he's putting himself in the jurors' minds.

They have to be thinking that he was there, they fought, his skin was under her fingernails. Then she wound up strangled to death.

How could they possibly not think he is guilty?

If we are allowed to present the defense I want, I think it's a good one.

The problem is that it's a reasonable-doubt case at its core, and we're up against a prosecution case based on incontrovertible science. That's not a great position for us to be in, but it's all we've got.

We are going to give the jury Arthur Wainwright as the alternative killer. But it's not necessary that the jury totally believes Wainwright is the guilty party. We're going to show them that all kinds of bad people are hovering over this case, and that many more murders have occurred. Then we're going to place Wainwright in their world.

Our evidence is not exactly ironclad, but we're just trying to convince one or two jurors. We just don't have the ammunition to get all twelve; the limited goal is to hang this jury and live to fight another day.

Part of me relishes this moment. After

playing defense throughout the trial, this is the time we get to go on the attack. We are in control of what happens over the next few days. It's much better to punch than to be punched.

But fear is there as well. If we, if I, don't get it done, then a person I believe to be innocent is going to be in prison for the rest of his life. I am not crazy about many things in lawyering, especially the intense work that comes with each and every case, but the worst part is this fear.

Speaking of worst parts, Hike comes over to help finalize our preparations. Once we've done that, Hike shakes his head and says, "No way the jury would buy this, but it's not going to matter. The judge won't let it in."

That's my Hike.

"The defense calls Laurie Collins."

Laurie stands up and walks to the stand. Every eye in the courtroom is on her, but she is used to that. When you look like Laurie, it's the rare eye that is not staring at you.

For all of the pressure of the moment, I'm reminded of the scene from *My Cousin Vinny* when Marisa Tomei as Mona Lisa Vito takes the stand. I half smile to myself as I expect to hear Laurie say, "You can't make those marks without positraction, which was not available on the Buick Skylark!"

I briefly take Laurie through her work history, the highlights of which are as a lieutenant in the Paterson Police Department, and as chief of police in her hometown of Findlay, Wisconsin. "What is your job now?" I ask.

"I'm a private investigator. Employed by you."

When I introduce a photograph of Freddie Siroka, Jenna asks if we can approach the bench. Once we do, she says, "Your Honor, before we go down this path, can we at least have a good faith showing that it's not a fishing expedition and is in fact relevant?"

"Your Honor," I say, "we will demonstrate relevance very quickly. And since Ms. Silverman has seen our discovery documents, she knows that as well as I do. I would respectfully suggest that she be proactively prevented from what are likely to be constant interruptions."

"Thank you, Mr. Carpenter, I deeply appreciate your advice on how to run my courtroom. I'll allow you to proceed for now, subject to your delivering on your promise to quickly demonstrate relevance."

I resume my questioning, asking Laurie if she has ever met Freddie Siroka, and she confirms that she has and gives the date of that meeting.

"Where did this take place?"

"At Hinchliffe Stadium, in the general area of where Kristen McNeil was killed. We were visiting the scene to gather information."

"Why was Mr. Siroka there?"

"We had determined that he had been following you. When we confronted him, he became violent. One of my fellow investigators subdued him, and then we detained and questioned him as to his motivation for doing the surveillance on you."

"Did he admit that he was in fact following me?"

She nods. "He did."

"Did he say why?"

"He said that he was hired by a Mr. George Taillon to do so, and that it was in reference to the Kristen McNeil case."

Jenna does not bother making a hearsay objection because she knows what's coming. She's heard the tape as part of discovery.

"Are you positive you are relating the substance of what he said accurately?"

"I am. I surreptitiously made a tape of it as he was talking."

I introduce the tape as evidence, in addition to an affidavit from our voice expert, a professor at Rutgers, that it is in fact Siroka. He has compared the voice on the tape to the voice on Siroka's voice mail. "Our expert is in the courtroom if Your Honor wishes to hear from him directly," I say.

Neither Judge Stiller nor Jenna considers it necessary; since the professor has already provided the affidavit, they both know what he will say. We play the tape, confirming all that Laurie had said.

"If you know, where is Mr. Siroka now?" I ask.

"He is dead."

"Natural causes?"

She shakes her head. "He was shot in the head."

Jenna starts her cross by asking if Laurie is familiar with Siroka's arrest and conviction history.

"Yes, I am."

"So you know about the nine arrests, four convictions, and three prison terms?"

"Yes."

"As a former police officer, did you find that you could rely on people with that kind of record to be truthful?"

"Sometimes they are, and sometimes they are not."

"I see," Jenna says. "I notice nowhere on that tape did Mr. Siroka say what the purpose was in following Mr. Carpenter. He just vaguely mentioned this case, but did not say what he or his employer had to gain by the surveillance. Is there something I missed?"

"I don't know what you missed or didn't miss," Laurie says, twisting the knife, "but you are correct that Siroka did not say that."

"Did he have listening equipment with him?"

"No."

"Binoculars? Night-vision goggles?"

"No and no."

"So he was just watching Mr. Carpenter as he went through his day?"

"Apparently."

"If Mr. Carpenter went to the supermarket, or the post office, Mr. Siroka would report that?"

"I don't know what he would report or not report."

"You said your other investigator subdued him, and then you questioned him. Is that correct?"

"That is correct."

"Is it possible that he feared being subdued even harder if he didn't come up with a story for you?"

"I don't know what was going through his mind. But as you heard on the tape, we did not threaten him."

"Thank you. No further questions."

Jenna has done an effective job on cross, but we still did well by having the jury hear a tape of Siroka admitting that the surveillance was related to this case. Had Laurie not made the tape, our case would be com-

ing to a screeching halt right now.
   But instead we move on.

Kyle Wainwright has gone back and forth since his conversation with Jeremy Kennon.

His decision was whether to tell his father that Carpenter might be coming after him. Kennon had said he wasn't sure; he admitted it was possible he misread the signals that Carpenter might or might not have been sending.

But Kennon was a smart guy whom Kyle respected, so he figured chances were good he was right. Carpenter might be intent on slandering Arthur Wainwright in a very public way, accusing him at least indirectly of having an affair with Kristen and maybe even being involved in her murder.

Kyle's relationship with his father had been checkered at best. Kyle respected Arthur's intelligence and his accomplishments. But on some level Kyle considered him a fraud, especially for his charitable efforts. He believed Arthur wanted to look good, rather than do good.

Arthur had sold his expensive home in an exclusive Englewood Cliffs neighborhood when his second wife passed away. He had divorced Kyle's mother when Kyle was ten years old, a defining event in Kyle's life because of how bitter the divorce was and how little his mother was left with. She had since died as well, leaving Kyle with no mother and a lot of resentment toward his father.

Arthur took a penthouse apartment in a Fort Lee building, with a spectacular view of Manhattan. It was easier for him to manage, and closer to the office. He no longer had an outdoor and an indoor pool or a tennis court or a private gym. That was okay with him because he didn't swim or play tennis or exercise.

Kyle rarely came by; he had only visited three times in the two years Arthur had lived there. They saw each other in the office all the time, but their work life was much more interactive than their private life. Kyle doubted Arthur could pick his granddaughter out of a kiddie lineup.

Besides the personal aspect to the current situation, Kyle agreed with Kennon that a pressing business interest was here. Sliming Arthur's reputation, even if not proven, could be a major problem for NetLink with its clients. Kyle was someday going to inherit a controlling interest in the company, so he had a lot to protect.

So when Kyle called and said he was coming over to talk, Arthur knew that the subject was going to be significant. But he did not expect what was coming.

"Andy Carpenter is coming after you," Kyle said.

"Coming after me? What does that mean?"

"I'm not positive, but I think he's going to claim that you had an affair with Kristen, and —"

"That's insane!" Arthur screamed, showing more emotion than Kyle thought he had ever seen from him.

"I'm not finished. He might also be pointing to you as the killer."

"Where are you getting this from?"

"Jeremy. He had a conversation with Carpenter, and this is the feeling he got. He's not sure, but we thought you should know so you can be prepared."

"Just let him try it. He has no evidence. I will sue him for every dime he's ever made or ever will make. I will grind him into dust."

"He is a well-respected attorney; I don't think it's a good idea to underestimate him."

"Into dust. Into dust."

So Kyle left, having fulfilled his duty. He was not sorry he'd warned his father that Carpenter was going to be making the accusations.

He was also not sure that Carpenter wasn't right.

My next witness is Pete Stanton.

I know how much he hates testifying for the defense because he told me that if I made him do this, he would hunt me down after the trial, shoot me, and feed my body in pieces to a tank full of piranhas.

Pete and I are really good friends.

"Captain Stanton, did you hear the tape that was played earlier in this courtroom? The one that testimony demonstrated was the voice of Freddie Siroka?"

"Yes."

"Did you hear him say that he was hired by George Taillon to follow me?"

"Yes."

"Were you familiar with Taillon? Could you describe what you knew about him?"

"He was a known criminal for hire. He had a lengthy arrest record, but was a suspect in far more crimes than he was tried for. Witnesses had a way of disappearing or recanting."

"So a bad guy?"

Pete nods. "A bad guy."

"Did I come to see you to discuss both Taillon and Siroka?"

"Yes." Pete is testifying as if he is paying by the word.

"Why did I say I wanted to talk to you?"

"They had both been murdered the night before, and you said you had information about it that could be helpful to the police."

"Could you describe the circumstances of those murders, as you know them?"

"They were each shot in the head in Pennington Park and their bodies left there. They were discovered approximately twenty-four hours later."

"What information did I have for you?"

"You told me the circumstances of Siroka following you, and his mentioning Taillon as his employer. You basically described what was on the tape."

"Did you give me any information in return?"

"Yes. I told you that Taillon had an associate named Mitch Holzer, a known criminal who worked with Taillon. I warned you that he was dangerous, and that you should be careful if you attempted to talk to him."

"Did we have another conversation two

days later?"

"Yes."

"Who precipitated that conversation?"

"I did. I was hoping you might have information regarding the murder of Mitch Holzer."

"The Mitch Holzer we spoke about two days earlier?"

Pete nods. "Yes."

"He was murdered during the course of those two days?"

"Yes."

"What did I tell you in our second meeting?"

"That you had spoken to Holzer, and he had revealed to you that he believed that the person Taillon and Siroka were working for was a man named Arrant. Holzer believed that Arrant might have been the killer."

"Did you do any research into who Arrant might be?"

"Yes. His full name was Charles Arrant. He was wanted for a decade by Interpol, with arrest warrants in three European countries. He was wanted for murder and various serious financial crimes."

"Also a bad guy?"

Pete nods. "A very bad guy."

"All of these murders we have been talking about . . . Siroka, Taillon, and Holzer. Is Noah Traynor a suspect in any of them?"

"No."

"Because he has been in jail this entire time, awaiting trial?"

"That is correct."

I turn Pete over to Jenna, who feigns boredom with the whole thing, as if this is just something we need to get through before the jury can vote to convict Noah.

Her questions are brief and to the point. "All of these people you are talking about, Siroka, Taillon, Holzer, and Arrant, they are all likely murderers?"

"I can't be sure about all of them, but it's a decent bet," Pete says.

"In your experience, are murderers violent people?"

"Yes."

"And sometimes they die violently?"

"Sometimes."

"Did any of them have their skin fragments under the fingernails of Kristen McNeil?"

"No."

"Thank you."

"The defense calls Corey Douglas," I say.

Corey comes to the stand. For him, a cop for many years, testifying in a trial is nothing close to new.

I take him through his work history, his recent retirement, and his work for us as an investigator. He also talks about Simon, and their work and personal life together. I'm quite sure that at least some members of the jury must have seen coverage of the hearing in which we secured Simon's early retirement.

Within ten minutes, I've turned Corey's attention to the night I was walking in the park with Tara and Sebastian. "You were there watching out for me? Protecting me?"

He nods. "Yes. You were not aware of it."

"Can you describe what happened?"

"An assailant was lying in wait for you in the park. He was preparing to shoot you, so I ordered Simon to attack him. Simon subdued him, and I was able to get his gun. I ordered him to stand and turn around, so that I could handcuff him."

"Did he obey your orders?"

"He started to, but he had another concealed weapon that he revealed and attempted to fire at me. I shot him in self-defense, and the wound was fatal."

"Did you learn his identity?"

Corey nods. "Yes. His name was Charles Arrant."

"The Charles Arrant that Mitch Holzer mentioned to me? The Charles Arrant that was wanted by Interpol?"

Corey nods again. "One and the same."

I would judge the first day of the defense case to be a modest success.

First and most important, no objections were successfully lodged on admissibility grounds. We are definitely home-free on that front because from here on we will be talking more about Kristen McNeil.

We have shown the jury that a lot of murders have been committed around here, none of which Noah Traynor is responsible for. We have not made an ironclad connection between those murders and this case, but we've established a strong inference.

We need to drive that home.

Laurie, Ricky, and I have a nice dinner, during which murders and trials are not mentioned. I'm feeling bad that I haven't been spending as much time with Ricky as I should; I rationalize it to myself that I am busy trying to prevent Danny Traynor from never spending time with his own father again.

After dinner the phone rings and Laurie answers it. She tells me that it is Herbert Hauser on the phone. I've never met Hauser, but I know of him. He's a corporate attorney and litigator, probably the most successful in New Jersey.

I no sooner say hello than he starts to unload on me. "It has come to my attention that you are preparing to slander my client Arthur Wainwright in open court."

I suspect that Jeremy Kennon told Wainwright of this possibility, and he freaked out. "Let me guess. You're calling to warn me against doing that."

"That is exactly correct. Mr. Wainwright has many options to deal with this kind of disgraceful behavior, and I will personally see to it that he uses them to maximum effect."

"Could you repeat that? I can barely hear you, what with my heart pounding and my knees knocking."

"You are obviously living up to your reputation. But you should think long and hard before you slander Mr. Wainwright."

This guy is really on my nerves. "Is this what you called to tell me, or do you have something to say that I give a shit about?"

"You have been warned, Mr. Carpenter."

Click.

When I get off, Laurie asks, "What was that about?"

"Wrong number."

I'm not worried about the threats from Arthur's lawyer.

I will simply be presenting evidence in open court, and every bit of it will be true and accurate. No one is going to perjure themselves. So I will not spend another moment thinking about that.

Much more concerning to me is that I don't have much to tie Arthur Wainwright or anyone else to the actual murder of Kristen McNeil. I've just got to get at least one person on the jury to believe me.

Once I'm done doing what I can to provide reasonable doubt, I'm going to have to make the key decision of the trial, the key decision of every trial: whether to have the defendant testify.

I can't remember the last time I encouraged a defendant to testify. It brings with it enormous risks. Usually the potential upside doesn't nearly justify doing it, but this case might just be the exception to that rule.

We simply have to give the jury an explanation for the DNA evidence, especially the skin and blood under Kristen's fingernails. No matter what else we present, no matter who we potentially implicate, that evidence will ultimately carry the day if not explained.

So I am not going to make a recommendation until I have to, and as always it will be the defendant's choice, but right now I am leaning toward urging Noah to testify.

Today is "Laurie day" in that our next two witnesses are people that Laurie has found through diligent investigating. They won't make our case for us, but they might provide important building blocks.

The first witness is Marlene Simms, who retired six years ago from her position as director of human resources at NetLink Systems. Simms is currently living in Florida; Laurie interviewed her over the phone and told me it would be worthwhile to fly her up to testify.

I tend to do what Laurie tells me.

I quickly establish the basics of Simms's career, with special attention on the twelve years she spent at NetLink. "So you were at NetLink Systems when Kristen McNeil was employed there?"

Simms nods. "Yes, sir."

"How did she come to get the job?"

"Well, it was an open secret that her boyfriend was Kyle Wainwright. Kyle's father, Arthur, is the founder and majority owner of NetLink. I'm assuming that's how the connection was made, though I can't say that for a fact."

"Did she have the kind of experience one would expect for the position?"

Simms thinks for a few moments. "That's hard to say. She had no experience whatsoever; she had just graduated high school. But the position had very little responsibility; she was an assistant who did relatively minor tasks."

"Who instructed you to hire her?"

"Arthur Wainwright."

I nod. "You said she was an assistant. Who did she assist?"

"Arthur Wainwright."

"Where was Kyle Wainwright during this time? Was he working at the company as well?"

"Yes, at least part time. I think he was getting ready to go to college, and even then he worked at NetLink during vacations. You can do that when your father owns the company."

"So is it fair to say that Kristen and Arthur Wainwright spent a lot of time together?"

Simms nods. "Oh, yes. She had a desk right outside his office. She took notes in his meetings, ran errands for him, those kind of things. He said it was a great way for her to learn the business. I'm sure that was true."

"Did she seem happy there? Ever express any complaints?"

"She seemed very happy; it was a great opportunity for her, and a nice place to work. But then suddenly she quit."

"Yes, let's talk about that. She came to you and said she was leaving?"

"No, she just didn't show up for work one day and called me from home. Said she was not coming back. She seemed very upset. I remember being stunned by it; it was so sudden, and I didn't expect it. As I said, she had seemed so happy. This came out of left field."

"Did she say why she was upset?"

Simms shakes her head. "No. I asked her if she wanted to come in and talk about it, but she was adamant that she did not want to do that. Usually when an employee leaves, we'd have an exit interview, but she wanted no part of that either."

"If you know, had she told Arthur Wainwright of her decision?"

"I can't say for sure, but I told her that he might want to speak to her directly, and she said, 'No, I'm not talking to him.' "

"You were surprised by that?"

"Very. Especially the way she said it. She blurted it out, but was decisive about it."

"As a professional who dealt with employees for many years, what was your overall impression of Kristen during that conversation?"

Simms pauses for a few moments, then a few moments more. I'm about ready to prompt her when she says, "She was upset, worried. . . . I would say she seemed scared. I have no explanation for why that would be the case."

Jenna objects that Simms couldn't know Kristen's state of mind. We argue the point and Judge Stiller comes down on my side, but it doesn't matter. The jury heard that Kristen was upset and afraid, and that she was adamant she would not talk to the person she was closest to at NetLink, Arthur Wainwright.

Next up is Mike Greer, who also worked at NetLink at the same time as Kristen. He started around the time that she did, but worked in finance.

"Did you have occasion to spend much time with her?" I ask.

He nods. "Some. We were both new there, so we were learning the ropes together. We'd go to lunch and talk about what it was like, and other stuff."

"Did you two date?"

He smiles. "No, I wanted to, but she said she wasn't really interested. She wanted to just be friends; that was pretty much the story of my life back then. She said her dating life was complicated enough. Then she said, 'Believe me, you have no idea how complicated.' "

"Did she seem happy at NetLink Systems?"

"Very. She wanted to make a career there. She even said she might take courses at night in the technical side of things, to really learn the basics of the business."

"Do you know why she quit?"

He shakes his head. "I will never understand that. One day she just wasn't there. I called her because I was worried about her. She said she was never coming back, but wouldn't say why. She didn't say she was scared, but she sounded like it."

I turn him over to Jenna, who again feigns indifference, as if this is all just a diversion from the conclusive DNA evidence.

Court is going to be closed for a couple of days, for New Year's Eve and New Year's

Day. "Happy New Year," I say to Noah as the guard takes him away.

"That remains to be seen," he says.

He's right about that.

It was going to be an agonizing day for Cynthia and Kevin McNeil.

There was simply no getting around that. They had put it off for fourteen long years, but that didn't matter at all. If they waited twenty more, the pain would be just as fresh.

This was the day they had decided they would go through Kristen's room. They would give most of her clothes, at least the ones that had survived the years intact, to charity. Other decisions, like what to do with her jewelry and other possessions, they would make in the moment. The deciding factors would be respect for Kristen, and what would hurt the least.

Karen, Kristen's sister and their lone remaining daughter, had come by to help get them through it. She thought they might back off at the last minute; they had come close on a few previous occasions but couldn't follow through. But this time they were committed; the New Year was going to be the start of reclaiming their own lives.

Or at least that was the plan.

So Karen came over, and they had breakfast together. They talked about Kristen but not the trial. Karen had attended every day and was planning to do so right through the verdict. But while her parents let her give them occasional reports, that wasn't the plan for today. Today they were not going to think about Kristen's death; they were going to focus on her life.

Then breakfast was over and the dishes were put away and there was no longer an excuse to delay. They took simultaneous deep breaths and entered Kristen's room.

It was completely clean and dust-free. Cynthia had cleaned it every day, even changing the bedding weekly. Kevin had occasionally joked that it had never been that clean when Kristen lived there, but Cynthia didn't think that was funny. Nor did Kevin.

So they went in with their plastic bags of various sizes, for the items that they would throw away, or give away, or keep. They made good progress; even though Kristen had accumulated a lot of stuff, it was still just one room, and they were three people.

Cynthia assigned herself the task of going through Kristen's desk drawers. She didn't think Kristen kept any kind of diary, but wasn't sure if she was right about that. It would be painful to read, but it would bring Kristen back in some small way, through her words.

No diary was found, but in the bottom drawer, or more accurately at the bottom of the bottom drawer, was a sealed letter-size envelope. On the outside it simply said, "Mother and Father."

Cynthia experienced a quick intake of air and intense anxiety as she reached for it. She opened it quickly, wanting to get whatever was about to happen over as soon as possible.

She read it and said three words aloud, to herself and to no one.

"Oh, my God."

I have a love/hate relationship with this holiday.

New Year's Eve is probably my least favorite day of the entire year, mainly because it leads into my least favorite night of the year. People all over the world get dressed up to go out to parties where they pretend to be wildly happy. They drink too much, eat too much, and then play DUI roulette as they drive home. The funny thing is that no actual fun is involved.

Even worse are the crowds that descend on Times Square to freeze their asses off, get their pockets picked, kiss diseased strangers, and cheer wildly at a falling six-ton piece of glass that doesn't even have the decency to break when it lands. Many of the poor slobs there would describe their last ten years as uniformly miserable, but somehow they always pretend the next one is going to be terrific, and it will start as soon as that stupid ball hits the ground.

Ricky has brought great joy to our lives in many ways, and New Year's Eve is just one of them. Laurie wants to spend the evening as a family, so we get to stay home and do family stuff. We play a board game or do a puzzle until Ricky falls asleep. Then Laurie wakes him to watch the ball drop.

The point is, we don't go out, which works well for me. And I have Ricky to thank for it.

New Year's Day is an entirely different animal. It is filled with college bowl games, six of them to be exact. They have not invented a bowl game that I won't watch. If the Salvation Army played the Little Sisters of the Poor in the Charity Bowl, I'd be glued to the television, and I'd probably bet on the game.

But New Year's Day has high-quality games; the teams that play have all had excellent seasons. Three of the games are on at roughly the same time, which makes it difficult, but I am one of the great remote-control artists of this era, so I cannot remember the last important play I missed.

But this weekend is nothing short of a football dream come true. That is because in addition to the great bowl games, Sunday brings an extraordinary NFL schedule. Not only that, but the Giants are playing the Redskins, and if the Giants win, they are in the playoffs, albeit it as a wild card. Then on Monday night are the collegiate national semifinal games, with the four best teams in the country.

Pinch me.

Of course, there is the trial to worry about, especially since our key witnesses are coming up. That means more trial prep today, so that I can watch football tomorrow and Sunday. The prep is probably overkill; I know the issues and details inside and out. I'm ready.

Football and the trial have an unusual and puzzling intersection. One of the calls on Arrant's burner phone was to the LSU defensive coordinator, Ben Walther. I still have no idea why Arrant made that call. Maybe the Feds have found out, but if it has had any legal repercussions for that coach, news of it has not hit the media. Which means it hasn't happened.

By three o'clock I am so sick of this trial preparation that I'm starting to wish I needed to leave for the Times Square festivities. I'm bored out of my mind. Laurie and Ricky are out shopping, Tara and Sebastian are asleep, and I have no one to talk to.

The phone rings and I grab it. I don't care

if it's a telemarketer; I'm going to strike up a conversation. Anything to stop me from having to go over these documents for the hundredth time.

I start it off with "Hello?," which is an old standby I often use to get the chitchat going.

"Mr. Carpenter?" It's a young woman's voice that I don't recognize, but I do detect the anxiety.

"Speaking."

"This is Karen McNeil. We met and . . ."

"I know who you are, Karen. Is everything all right?"

"No . . . I . . . I'm not sure. Can you come over here? It's very important."

"Of course. Where are you?"

"My parents' house. There is something here. . . . You need to see it."

She gives me the address, which is in Teaneck, and I tell her I'll be there in a half hour. I leave immediately and beat my half-hour prediction by three minutes.

The McNeils live on a cul-de-sac in a neighborhood of comfortable homes with manicured lawns. It presents a picture that would be in the dictionary next to *suburbia.* As I pull up in front, the door opens and Karen McNeil stands there. Behind her are two people I'm fairly confident are her parents.

I walk up to the porch, and Karen thanks me for coming and introduces me to Cynthia and Kevin as we walk in. We go into the kitchen, and Cynthia offers me coffee or something else to drink. I decline, and I sense that they are grateful for that. Whatever this is about, they want to get it over with in a hurry.

"How can I help you?" I say, a general question addressed to whoever wants to answer it.

Apparently Kevin is the designated answerer because he says, "Ever since Kristen left us, we haven't touched her things. Cynthia cleaned her room almost every day, but we left her possessions intact."

I already knew this; Karen had mentioned it to Laurie and me. But I don't reveal this, in case Karen might think I was throwing her under the bus. Instead I just nod and wait for Kevin to continue.

"We've thought about doing it many times, but never seemed to be able to. We decided to do it for the new year, especially with the arrest, and the trial ending soon. So today was the day."

"That must have been hard," I say.

He nods. "Maybe not for some people,

but very hard for us. Anyway, in the bottom drawer of Kristen's desk, she had hidden this." He takes an envelope off the kitchen counter and hands it to me. "Please open it and read it."

So I do.

The next thing I do is email Hike instructions on what we need to get done in a hurry. I don't want to call him because I don't want the McNeils to hear the conversation. Hike spends a lot of time on the computer surfing the Web, looking for bad news in the world wherever he can find it. He keeps our work email open as he does, so I hope he'll see this message quickly.

My instructions are for Hike to start assembling the necessary experts we'll need first thing Monday morning; the timing is going to be all-important.

The trial is about to be turned on its head.

I don't know if the letter that the McNeils found in Kristen's room is real, but I have no reason to doubt it. The court and the prosecution may have plenty of reason to doubt it, though, so we have spent the past twenty-four hours dealing with experts in the field.

I don't have the results yet, but Hike is not in court this morning so that he can receive them. Even Hike is confident that they will turn out in our favor, which I have to admit gives me pause.

A snowstorm is going on. It started last night and we've already gotten more than six inches. Amazingly, it has not deterred the public from filling every seat in the gallery. This trial has caught and held the public's attention.

I call Sergeant Lucy Alvarez to the stand. She is one of the officers working the

George Taillon murder. It's fair to say that the police are not mounting a full-court press to find the person who killed Taillon and Siroka since everyone believes that the guilty party is Charles Arrant, who is himself already dead.

To make matters simpler, I had asked her to familiarize herself with one specific aspect of the Charles Arrant murder case. The Paterson Police are not working it at all and barely paying lip service to it because with his Interpol warrants, the Feds came in and took over.

As I stand, I notice that Herbert Hauser, the lawyer that threatened me on Arthur Wainwright's behalf, is in the courtroom, notepad and pen in hand. No doubt his presence is to send me a message, since a transcript of the trial will be readily available to him after the fact. He didn't have to come here to learn what I say.

Color me intimidated.

"Sergeant Alvarez, you are familiar with Charles Arrant and the fact that he was shot to death?"

"Yes, though it is not my case."

"Did I ask you to acquire some information about it so that you could offer it in your testimony?"

"You didn't ask me. You asked Captain

Stanton and he instructed me to do it."

I smile. "Thank you for the correction. What did Captain Stanton instruct you to get?"

"There was a burner cell phone that was found in Mr. Arrant's hotel room at the Saddle Brook Marriott. He was registered under an assumed name."

"Where is that cell phone now?"

"I believe it remains in the custody of the FBI."

"Why the FBI?" I ask, pretending I don't know.

"There were three Interpol Red Notices out on him, which makes it a federal case."

"Did they tell you what phone calls had been made on that cell phone?"

"Yes."

I introduce the document the FBI had sent the Paterson Police, detailing the calls. Then, "Can you tell the jury who was called from that phone?"

"One call was to a video-game manufacturer in Oklahoma named Gameday. It was answered by the switchboard, so there is no way to know who the call was routed to. The second call was to a man named Ben Walther, who is a football coach at Louisiana State University."

The gallery mumbles on hearing that

name, possibly because it was completely unexpected, or maybe because LSU is playing tonight.

"And the third call?"

"He called George Taillon, who I believe you are familiar with."

I nod. "I am, but for those scoring at home, this is the George Taillon who ordered me followed, and who was himself murdered?"

She nods. "That's him."

"Thank you, Sergeant. And since we're on the subject, are you working the Taillon murder case?"

"I am."

"I subpoenaed phone records of Mr. Taillon, and I asked the phone company to get you copies. Is that correct?"

"Yes."

"Did you receive and review them?"

"Yes."

I ask her to focus on the calls that Taillon received, and direct her to the date of Kristen McNeil's death. She testifies that Taillon received two phone calls from burner phones the day before the murder, and one the night of the murder.

"Is that suspicious to you?" I ask.

"Perhaps, but there could be innocent explanations."

I nod as if that is reasonable, which it is. "Now please turn to the phone calls Mr. Taillon made during that period of time."

She does so, and I ask her to identify two specific calls with the same phone number. "When were those phone calls made, in reference to the death of Kristen McNeil?"

"One was made seven days prior to the murder, and the other five days prior."

"Who does that number belong to?"

"NetLink Systems."

"And did I ask you to call that number today?"

"You did, and I did so."

"Was it the NetLink switchboard?"

"No, it was the private line for Arthur Wainwright."

Just in case the jury is not paying close enough attention, I hammer the point home. "George Taillon called Arthur Wainwright's private line twice within a week of Kristen McNeil's murder?"

"That is correct."

I think the jury and everyone else in the courtroom realize the significance of this. What they don't realize is that they ain't heard nothin' yet.

I made the decision not to prep my next witness.

I basically told her what I was planning to ask, but did not request answers. I want the testimony to be completely spontaneous; it will be more powerful that way.

I spend the lunch hour going over the material Hike has come back with. I have to listen to him complain about how slippery the roads are from the snow, and how he almost got killed twice. Once we're past that, he reveals that as both he and I expected, the information he's gotten fits exactly with what we hoped for. Now all I have to plan is how to introduce it to the judge and prosecution.

Before the jury is brought into the courtroom to take their seats, I ask the judge if we could briefly meet in his chambers, lead counsel only. He agrees, and Jenna and I follow him back there. Jenna looks warily at me, for good reason.

"Your Honor, these are copies of a letter, written by the victim in this case, that I am going to introduce into evidence. The witness who will be testifying is Karen McNeil, Kristen's sister." Since Karen, Cynthia, and Kevin McNeil were all present when the letter was found, I gave them the option of which of them would testify. Karen won the vote, three to zero.

The judge and Jenna take a few moments to read the letter, and Jenna is clearly stunned. "Your Honor, this is outrageous. The defense is claiming that this letter has existed for fourteen years, and they are springing it on us five minutes before the jury would hear it, without having shared it in discovery, as is their obligation?"

"Your Honor, I say, we have only had it for less than —"

Jenna interrupts, "And it is not even authenticated. Anyone could have written this at any time."

"Thank you for making my point for me," I say. "Your Honor, we had concerns about its authenticity as well, so we took great pains, at significant expense, to have its legitimacy confirmed by top experts. We are prepared to present their affidavits to that effect, and they are here in the courtroom available to testify if necessary.

"The salient point is that we literally received their verdicts within the last two hours, far too late to turn it over in discovery. I wish that were not the case, but we did everything properly and by the book."

Judge Stiller has two options here. There is no chance he will disallow the letter; he could never prevent blockbuster evidence like this from reaching the jury. He'd be overturned on appeal before the ink on the verdict form was dry. His two choices are to let the trial move forward now, or to grant a continuance to give the prosecution time to study it. I hope he chooses the former, but I can live with either one.

He surprises me by splitting the difference and coming up with a third choice. He says that we can move forward, but after the testimony, he will grant the prosecution a delay until tomorrow if they want the time to prepare for cross-examination. It seems to me like a reasonable compromise; not so much to Jenna.

We head back into the courtroom, the jury is called in, and Karen McNeil takes the stand. "We're calling her?" asks Noah, surprised that the victim's sister might be a witness for the defense.

I thought about giving him a heads-up on

what is going to happen, but decided against it. Let him enjoy it as it unfolds.

As I stand, I notice that Cynthia and Kevin McNeil are in the gallery for the first time. They are coincidentally sitting next to Hauser, Arthur Wainwright's lawyer, who, I have a feeling, is about to put away his notepad.

I introduce Karen and have her talk briefly about her relationship to Kristen: "We were very close, in age and every other way. We were best friends. I still miss her every single minute of every single day."

"Did Kristen ever mention Noah Traynor to you?"

Karen shakes her head. "No, she didn't."

"What did you do this past Saturday?"

"I went to my parents' house."

"Why?"

"My parents haven't gone through Kristen's room in all these years. They cleaned it, but never moved or touched her things. They treated it like a shrine; they couldn't bring themselves to do anything else."

"Was Saturday significant in that regard?"

Karen nods. "They decided to do it, to start the new year fresh. This trial was going to be the turning point that would allow them to move on, or at least as much as was possible. They would be the first to admit that after losing a child, nothing is ever the same."

"And you were there to help?"

Karen nods. "And support them, yes."

"Please describe what happened."

"Well, we were going through her things, deciding what we wanted to give to charity, what to keep for sentimental reasons . . . that kind of thing. Then my mother started going through her desk drawers, and she found an envelope." Karen is starting to choke up as she says this; her emotion and distress are real and palpable.

"Do you want a minute?"

She shakes her head. "No, I want to get through this."

I go back to the defense table and pick up the envelope and introduce it officially as evidence. Then I hand it to Karen. "Is this it?"

"It certainly looks like it."

"Please open it and take out what is inside."

She does as instructed and unfolds the piece of paper.

"Please read it."

She looks at it and starts to read. " 'Mother and Father, if you're reading this . . .' " She stops and starts to sob softly. Then, "I'm sorry. . . . I . . ."

"Would it be easier if the clerk read it for you?"

"No . . . I'm sorry. . . . I'll be okay." Karen lifts up the letter and starts to read again. " 'Mother and Father, if you're reading this, then you know I have left home. Please don't try to find me or contact me; it would put all of us in danger. I have saved a good amount of money, so don't worry about me. . . . I can take care of myself. I have had an affair with Arthur Wainwright, but that is not why I have left. It is because I have learned something terrible about him. He knows that I know, and I'm afraid of what he will do. I'm sorry . . . please try to understand.' " Then, "She signed it, 'Love you forever, Kris.' "

The silence in the courtroom is deafening. I turn and see that Cynthia and Kevin are quietly sobbing, which does not make them unique in the gallery. Herbert Hauser has, in fact, put away his notepad.

I introduce the affidavits certifying the authenticity of the letter. We have had a handwriting expert confirm that it is Kristen's writing and a carbon-dating expert confirm by analyzing the ink and paper that it was written well more than a decade ago. He can't confirm that it was exactly fourteen years, but says that is certainly possible, even likely.

Jenna opts not to delay her cross-examination until tomorrow. I think it's a correct decision; she wants this testimony over as soon as possible. She has no way to damage Karen and would look bad doing so even if she could, since Karen is so obviously sympathetic.

All she can do is confirm that Karen and Kristen were close and then get her to say that Kristen never revealed an affair with Arthur Wainwright to her. It is ineffective at best because Kristen also never revealed anything about Noah Traynor to Karen either.

When I get back to the defense table, Noah obeys my pretrial admonition not to show emotion, good or bad. He must be jumping out of his skin with happiness, but he's hiding it.

I know the feeling. Defense attorneys don't get many days like this; if we did, I would like working more.

I can't get overconfident about this.

We still have a major hill to climb. In our favor is that Kristen, in her own written words, said that she was having an affair with Arthur Wainwright and that she was running away because he presented a deadly danger.

That is incredibly compelling, but it doesn't prove that Arthur did anything. Kristen's fear could have been misplaced; maybe Arthur did not pose a real threat to her at all. Or maybe he did but never acted on it.

It is balanced by the fact that ironclad evidence shows Noah Traynor had been at the scene of the crime and had left his blood and skin under Kristen's fingernails.

I think we still have to attack this evidence, to tell an alternative story about it, different than the prosecution's. The only way to do that is to have Noah testify.

I have an instinctive revulsion at the idea of a defendant taking the stand, but that's what I am going to recommend here. Fortunately, I have had Hike prepping Noah on the testimony he will give. He wants to do it, and Hike says Noah should do okay. For Hike that is a five-star review.

I cannot imagine what is going through Arthur Wainwright's mind tonight. Yesterday he was a well-respected businessman and community leader. Today he has been credibly accused of having an affair with an eighteen-year-old employee, then murdering her to protect some terrible secret that she learned about him.

Not a good day for old Artie.

The media is obviously covering the hell out of the day's events, but I am focused on something that they are not. Kristen said in her letter that Arthur was concealing a terrible secret. It wouldn't be just the affair; it had to be something else. But what? Whatever that is, it is most likely the same secret that Arrant has been murdering to protect.

Hike is going down to the jail tonight to meet with Noah one more time and prep him again for his testimony. He will also confirm that Noah still wants to do it; it is totally his call.

Tonight I am going to go over the mechanics of my side of it. I'm pretty well prepared already, so I'll take some time to watch the LSU-Clemson game and wonder what the LSU defensive coordinator could possibly have had to do with Charles Arrant.

Tomorrow I am going to call two character witnesses, friends of Noah's, and then Noah himself. Then I will rest our case.

Big day tomorrow.

Hike and I are sitting at the defense table when Noah is brought in.

He looks nervous, which makes perfect sense. I wish I knew more about Noah; I wish I knew whether he rises to the occasion under pressure or wilts in the face of it. I'm going to find out that answer at the same time everyone else in the courtroom will.

"You feeling okay?" I ask.

He takes a deep breath. "Yeah, I am. I'm looking forward to it."

I nod. "Good. You'll do fine."

The bailiff tells us to rise as the judge enters. Then he says whatever he thinks necessary and has the jury brought in. Judge Stiller is prompt and has never kept us waiting.

Until today.

Today fifteen minutes go by with no Judge Stiller. It's almost like he's a coach calling time-out to ice the kicker about to make the pressure kick; in this case the "kicker" under pressure is Noah. But there is no chance that is happening; something else is going on.

When the fifteen-minute delay stretches to twenty-five, something significant must undoubtedly be causing this. Sure enough, the clerk comes out of the back where the judge's chambers are and walks over to first Jenna and then me.

"The judge wants to speak with you in chambers, immediately," the clerk says.

As we follow the clerk, Jenna and I make eye contact. The look on her face says that she has no more idea what is going on than I do.

The judge is sitting at his desk in street clothes, which in itself is highly unusual. He always looks serious, at least when he's working, but this time he looks positively somber.

"Sit down," he says. "Please."

Jenna and I sit down across from him and do the only thing we can do. We wait.

"I received some information about forty-five minutes ago," Stiller says. "I've attempted to confirm what I could, but some of the details are still unclear. But here is what we know for sure."

He takes a deep breath. "At some time during the night before last, probably between midnight and four A.M., Arthur Wainwright drove to a cemetery in Little Falls. He went to his former wife's gravesite, sat next to the headstone, put a handgun in his mouth, and fired it. He died instantly."

Judge Stiller's words just hang in the air, as Jenna and I sit in stunned silence. We don't say anything because neither of us knows what to say.

Judge Stiller picks up the slack. "The reason it took more than twenty-four hours to discover the body is apparently due to the snow that fell on it, plus it was in a secluded area of the cemetery.

"You are going to have differing views on how this news will or should impact this trial. I suspect that you, Mr. Carpenter, will feel strongly that the jury hear about it. Ms. Silverman, I'm not going too far out on a limb to say that you will oppose that.

"I also suspect that however it is handled it will impact the manner in which you end your case, Mr. Carpenter. So here is what I have decided to do. Court will not be in session today; we will resume tomorrow. I am going to sequester the jury, effective immediately.

"Depending on how we proceed, that

sequestration will either be for one night or the duration of the trial. So prepare your arguments, file written briefs before the close of business today, and I will see you back here tomorrow morning for oral arguments."

Holy shit.

I know I am going to spend the rest of the day and night preparing my arguments for getting this news in front of the jury, and also deciding whether, if I am successful, I'll still want Noah to testify.

But in the immediate aftermath of hearing the news, that's not what is dominating my mind. What I am feeling is . . . guilt.

Arthur Wainwright did not kill himself because of what I did in court yesterday. That could not have happened because he died before Karen testified about the letter. So either his decision was as a result of what I did in court prior to yesterday, or he somehow found out about the letter in advance of my presenting it.

Either way, I know intellectually that I did nothing wrong, and I also know that I only introduced evidence that was 100 percent true and accurate.

But the other fact that is 100 percent true and accurate is that I caused the death of Arthur Wainwright.

Hike handed in our brief yesterday afternoon, moments before the prosecution submitted theirs.

The issue in front of us is whether to tell the jury about Arthur Wainwright's suicide. I'm sure the jurors know that something important is going on because they were suddenly sequestered last night.

Obviously our defense position is that they should be told, but in addition to wanting that to happen, I also think it's the right thing to do.

We're about to be called into the judge's chambers for oral arguments, and I'm concerned about how Judge Stiller might rule. If he was leaning toward letting it in, I am surprised that he wouldn't have just done so yesterday. That he didn't and instead chose the major step of isolating those jurors indicates to me that he must be seriously considering leaving them in the dark.

As Jenna and I are walking toward the judge's chambers, Jenna asks me softly, "What do you think?"

"I think it's fifty-fifty. Maybe sixty-forty in your favor. What about you?"

"Fifty-fifty sounds about right."

As soon as we're seated and the court reporter is ready, Judge Stiller says for the record who is present, where we are meeting, and what the issue under discussion is. Then, "Let's hear from the prosecution first."

"Thank you, Your Honor. Our position is that this news is far more prejudicial than it is probative. The jurors will draw an inference that the suicide is directly related to this trial, and we do not know that to be the case. Even if we did know that for sure, we do not know why he did it. Maybe it was just the embarrassment of being accused, or of it being revealed that he had an affair with an eighteen-year-old girl. Maybe he was dealing with incredible, unrelated stress, or a serious health issue, and this development just pushed him over the edge.

"Arthur Wainwright is not here to defend his actions with Ms. McNeil, assuming she was telling the truth in her note, or explain the reason that he took his own life. We don't have anywhere near the knowledge or information to make the explanation for him.

"We would be entering unchartered waters here, and we cannot take a dead man with us. He cannot speak for himself, and we cannot speak for him. As I said, attempting to do so would be prejudicial to the extent that it would far exceed the probative value."

Stiller nods and turns to me. "Mr. Carpenter?"

"Your Honor, with respect, Ms. Silverman effectively makes our point. There are a number of potential explanations for Mr. Wainwright's suicide besides the one that she fears, that he killed himself because he has been revealed as the person who murdered Kristen McNeil. Embarrassment, stress, medical issues . . . every one of those and more are conceivably correct, and she is free to make the jury aware of all of them. We can take our own position, and then the jury can decide. That is their proper role.

"As of two days ago, Arthur Wainwright was a person that we might well have called to the stand. Now he is the ultimate unavailable witness. We are therefore damaged by his absence; you would further damage us by denying us the ability to explain the reason for that absence.

"Jurors might wonder why we are not calling him. Are we afraid to confront him and hear his effective defense? Absent information, they will draw their uninformed conclusions. Yet we have the power to inform them.

"There is a very significant precedent for our position, and —"

Judge Stiller interrupts, "Case law?"

"In a way. I am talking about this case, and the precedent that you have already set. You have admitted testimony about the deaths of four people, Siroka, Taillon, Holzer, and Arrant, including the circumstances of those deaths. I believe that those people are related to this case, and that you were correct to admit that evidence.

"But Arthur Wainwright is far more clearly a factor in this case. He has arguably been accused of the murder by the victim herself. To admit that other testimony, and then to keep this out, would be totally inconsistent and I believe ill-advised.

"This is a search for the truth. The jury needs to hear the facts, and then we can put our spin on them to try and convince them of our point of view. To deprive them of this key fact is to set up an artificial barrier to arriving at that truth."

We argue it out a bit more, but the issues have been laid out, both orally and in the briefs. Judge Stiller doesn't interrupt any more, and when we are finally finished, he simply says, "It comes in."

We go back into the courtroom, and I give a slight nod to Hike and Noah to let them know we have prevailed. Then I call Sergeant Stan Frazier of the Little Falls Police Department, who I have arranged to have here in case the judge ruled in our favor. If we are going to tell the story to the jury, we need a witness to do so.

I don't beat around the bush; this will be more effective if I make it short and sweet. I ask Frazier to describe what he found when he was called to the cemetery.

"A deceased male, age sixty-one. Cause of death was an apparently self-inflicted gunshot wound."

"Were you able to identify the deceased?"

Frazier nods. "Yes. It was Arthur Wainwright."

"Thank you."

It's decision time regarding Noah's possible testimony.

The advantage to his doing so is clear. His words are the only way to explain to the jury why he was at Hinchliffe Stadium that day, and more important, how his skin and blood wound up under Kristen McNeil's fingernails.

The jury is going to want to know that.

But the other factor is the manner in which I want to end the defense case. Frazier's testimony, brief as it was, was incredibly dramatic. The apparent importance of it was even inadvertently increased by Judge Stiller's decision to sequester the jury last night.

By doing so he was saying to them that something important had happened, so important that they had to be protected from knowing it. Now they know it, and I don't see how they can look past it. The victim made the accusation from the grave, and the accused reacted to it by killing himself. Surely that would have to put a reasonable doubt about Noah's guilt in the mind of a juror.

The alternative to this dramatic ending would be to have Noah testify. No matter how well he held up, the last thing the jury would see and hear would be Jenna badgering him, pointing out holes in his story, and reminding the jury that he kept quiet for fourteen years.

That would have the effect of ending on the prosecution's terms, and putting more time and space between their deliberations and the impact of hearing about Wainwright's death.

My assessment is that to end it here insures us of at least a hung jury, with an outside chance for an acquittal. Noah's testimony would be a roll of the dice, increasing the odds of either a conviction or outright acquittal, according to how he did and whether the jury believed him.

When a defendant testifies, it takes all the air out of the room. It dominates the trial, positively or negatively. I don't want Noah Traynor's words to dominate this trial. I want the trial to be dominated by Arthur Wainwright's actions.

This is about risk and reward. But even more than that, it's about instinct and trusting my gut. The problem is that my gut doesn't seem to have a point of view on this, and it's deferring to my brain.

At this crucial moment, my gut is gutless.

I lean across to Noah. "I don't think you should testify."

He nods. "Okay."

"But as I've told you before, it's your call."

He nods. "My call is to trust your judgment."

"Call your next witness, Mr. Carpenter."

"Your Honor, the defense rests."

Laurie has been in the gallery today; we drove here together in the morning. On the way home, she says, "I think you made the right decision in not having Noah testify. The pressure on him would be unbearable, and even though he'd be telling the truth, Jenna could have made him look bad."

"If you thought I made the wrong decision, would you tell me?"

"No chance."

I laugh for the first time in a while.

Tonight I'm going to prepare for my closing statement, which will not be hard to do. For one thing, the entire trial is always one long preparation for my closing statement. For another, I never write out a speech like some lawyers do. I list in my mind the bullet points I want to cover, but that's it. I've long ago learned that I am best when I'm spontaneous.

That will give me plenty of time to think about Arthur Wainwright, who reacted solely to what Andy Carpenter said and did just days before by going to a cemetery and swallowing his gun. It seems amazing to me that the testimony I brought out before revealing Kristen's letter could have been enough to push him over the edge. I'm starting to believe he must have found out about the letter well before Karen McNeil's testimony about it in court.

In any event, Arthur's suicide is an image I am not going to be able to remove from my imagination anytime soon, if ever.

The media is all over the story; a prominent citizen such as Arthur Wainwright committing suicide would be big news even if there was not a trial. With the circumstances as they are, everyone is opining on exactly what happened. Most believe that his killing himself was a direct result of my trial efforts.

My retirement is going well.

At eight o'clock I am completely ready for court tomorrow and need to take my mind off things, so I head down to Charlie's.

Vince and Pete are at our regular table, which is not exactly a news event. If they weren't here, it would be grounds to put out an all-points bulletin.

"Well, look who's here," Pete says. "And in the middle of a trial?"

I nod as I take my seat. "I've been dealing with so many important things, I need to take a break and hear some mindless drivel. Obviously I thought of the two of you."

"Why must you hurt us?" asks Vince, not once taking his eyes off the nearest television. It's a football game between Jacksonville and Tampa Bay, and if Vince cares about it, it means he has a bet on it.

"I am never testifying for you again," Pete says. "It's embarrassing; nobody at the precinct will even talk to me."

"Arthur Wainwright found a way to avoid it," I say.

"Were you going to call him?" Pete asks.

"No, but he had no way of knowing that. Did he leave a note?"

"You pumping me for information?"

"Obviously. Did he leave a note?"

"No."

"But you're sure it was a suicide?"

"No, he put the gun in his mouth, but he was just trying to wound himself."

"You know what I mean."

He nods. "Fingerprints on the gun; no indication anyone else was present. Nothing is ever definite, but the coroner didn't agonize over how to categorize it."

I realize that no matter where I go or what I do, I can't escape thinking about this case. "Let me ask you a question," I say to Pete. "What the hell was Charles Arrant, international criminal wanted by Interpol . . . what the hell was he doing in Paterson?"

"I have been asking myself that same question. I wish I had an answer."

I nod. "Next question. Whatever he was doing here . . . with him gone, you think someone took his place?"

Pete answers with a question of his own. "Are you thinking that same someone killed Arthur Wainwright and made it look like a suicide?"

"Not really, but part of me hopes it's true."

"Why?"

"Because if someone else didn't kill Wainwright, then I did."

"Here's what we know beyond a shadow of a doubt," Jenna says.

She has spent most of the trial asking questions from a podium set up between the defense and prosecution tables, but now she is pacing around as she begins her closing argument.

"Noah Traynor was with Kristen McNeil outside of Hinchliffe Stadium, the place where she was brutally murdered. We know this because his DNA was on a piece of discarded gum and a beer can.

"We don't know how much he had to drink that day, or how much alcohol might have affected his actions. Of course, the police couldn't measure his blood-alcohol level because he hid from them for fourteen years.

"We also know that Kristen and Noah Traynor had a violent confrontation; she scratched him so hard that she had his skin and blood under her fingernails. That could not have been done casually; that had to have been done in desperation.

"That would be less important if Kristen McNeil was shot from a distance, but she wasn't. She was murdered in as personal a way as one can be murdered. Her killer wrapped his arms around her neck and squeezed so violently that in addition to depriving her of the air she needed to survive, he broke her neck and crushed her larynx in the process.

"We don't have to have been there to imagine that while it was happening, she was clawing and scratching at her killer's arms, trying to get him off of her." Jenna pauses for effect. "Clawing and scratching . . . digging her nails into him.

"It's also important to remember another incontrovertible fact. Noah Traynor hid from the police for fourteen years. He could have said, 'I was there. I want to help find the real killer. Ask me any questions you have.' But he did not. Do you think that is the way an innocent man would react?

"Mr. Carpenter responded to this evidence by basically leaving it unchallenged. That was wise on his part because it would have been futile to try and attack it. So instead he paraded a veritable hit parade of unsavory characters in front of you, none of whom had anything to do with this case. I half expected him to bring up Al Capone and Osama bin Laden. But all he was trying to do was distract you, plain and simple.

"That brings me to Arthur Wainwright. Kristen McNeil wrote a letter to her parents about him. You read it. It says that she had an affair with him and that she was running away because she was frightened of him.

"Let's assume she was telling the truth; I have no reason to doubt her sincerity. Is it not possible she was afraid of him because he was wealthy and successful, a man capable of exercising tremendous influence in the community? Could she not have feared that he could hurt her and her parents, not physically, but financially, or reputationally?

"But maybe not. Maybe she thought he might physically attack her. That is a huge leap from his actually doing it. It was not his skin under her fingernails, and there is absolutely no evidence, not a shred of it, that places him at Hinchliffe Stadium that day.

"And speaking of no evidence, there is no evidence that Arthur Wainwright, who was forty-seven years old at the time of Kristen's death, had ever committed a violent act in his life.

"But three nights ago, he did commit a violent act, the ultimate violent act, against himself. I am certain that Mr. Carpenter will tell you that he did so out of guilt, or shame, all as the result of his being exposed as a murderer. But maybe he was ashamed at being revealed as someone who had an affair with a teenager. Or maybe he had a serious illness, or crisis in his life, and this was just the last straw?

"We can't get inside the mind of a tormented man. We have to focus on what we know. And we know, through evidence that simply cannot be refuted, that Noah Traynor killed Kristen McNeil.

"Thank you for listening, and thank you very much for your service."

My turn.

I also pace the room as I talk, just as I do when questioning witnesses. I begin with "Freddie Siroka. George Taillon. Mitch Holzer. Charles Arrant. These were all people that had violent criminal histories. You heard that from none other than the man in charge of the Homicide Division of the Paterson Police Department, Captain Pete Stanton.

"They were all connected to this case. You also heard that from Captain Stanton, and in one case you even heard it from Freddie Siroka, on audiotape. And they were all murdered, except for Mr. Arrant, who was killed while trying to murder yours truly.

"Noah Traynor is not a suspect in any of these murders. He has the perfect alibi; he was sitting in jail after being wrongly arrested for the death of Kristen McNeil.

"And then there is Arthur Wainwright. He was having a sexual relationship with a girl who was of an age where she could have been his daughter. In fact, she was the girlfriend of his son. You didn't have to hear this from me, you read it from Kristen McNeil's own hand.

"She feared him; she was petrified at what he might do. So much so that she quit the job that she loved, and she was running away, leaving friends and family behind. Again, those are not my words, they are hers.

"I want to talk for a moment about reasonable doubt. The judge will tell you that if you have a reasonable doubt as to whether or not Noah Traynor is guilty, then you must vote not guilty. That's clear and it is the foundation on which this system is based.

"If you think it is possible that someone else other than Noah Traynor committed this crime, then by definition you have reasonable doubt. So let me present you with a hypothetical situation:

"Supposing you heard from someone, maybe two or three people, that you completely trust . . . and they were to tell you that Arthur Wainwright killed Kristen McNeil. Maybe they even saw it happen, maybe not. But they were positive that they were right.

"What would your reaction be? Would you say, 'That's crazy . . . absolutely impossible?' Would you tell them that they're nuts, that Wainwright could not have done it?

"I don't think you would. I think that after hearing the evidence, and especially the letter that Kristen McNeil wrote, that it would make sense to you. You might not fully believe it, you might not be certain of it, but you'd certainly think it was possible.

"I believe what Kristen McNeil wrote, and I believe Arthur Wainwright killed himself because the truth was revealed. And if you think there is a chance that I am right, then you must have a reasonable doubt as to Noah Traynor's guilt.

"And if you have that reasonable doubt, you must vote to acquit. That is your responsibility.

"Thank you."

I think the likely outcome will be a hung jury.

I would never say that out loud to Laurie or Hike or Noah; it would violate one of my superstitions, which is to never verbalize a prediction of any kind about a verdict.

My reason for thinking so is pretty simple. I cannot imagine every single juror hearing the evidence about Arthur Wainwright, and knowing about his suicide, thinking there is not reasonable doubt as to Noah's guilt.

On the other hand, I also cannot imagine every single juror saying that it is a coincidence that Noah's skin was under the victim's fingers, but someone else killed her.

The great majority of trials end in convictions, more than 70 percent, so usually the defense is pleased with a hung jury. It keeps them alive to fight another day, and the prosecution might not choose to retry it.

That's not how I view this case. We caught

every break; the letter from Kristen was found at a perfect time for us: just in time for us to present it, but too late for the prosecution to prepare for it.

As tragic as it was, Wainwright's suicide was also perfectly placed in the chronology of the trial, especially for dramatic effect. If we have a second trial, we would lose that advantage. In the interim, it could also turn out that he had other things going on in his life that contributed to his final, fatal decision.

So it's time for me to go into my weird zone, where I obey a hundred different superstitions, all of them stupid. For example, I only get out of bed during a verdict watch when the digital clock's time ends with an odd number. I won't make left turns while I'm driving, no matter what.

I also won't use the treadmill or exercise bike. Okay, I tell Laurie that those are superstitions, but I'm lying. I don't use the treadmill and exercise bike because I hate the treadmill and exercise bike.

During a verdict wait, I become surly, obnoxious, and a torture to be around. Even Tara has little patience for me; she hangs around with Laurie far more than normal.

One thing I never do is look at any of the trial documents, and I try to think about the facts of the case as little as possible. To do otherwise would be to cause me to second-guess my decisions; there will be plenty of time to do that after the verdict, if it goes against us.

Because I think the jury will ultimately be hung, I think that by definition they will take a long time to deliberate. I would think they will eventually tell the judge they're deadlocked, and he'll send them back to try harder. This could happen two or three times.

We're only in the third day of deliberations now, so while I don't think a verdict is imminent, I stay by the phone that I doubt will ring.

So of course it rings.

And of course it's Rita Gordon, the court clerk. "Judge Stiller wants you down here now."

"Is there a jury issue?"

She laughs a short laugh. "Yeah, you might say there's a jury issue, Andy. They've reached a verdict."

I've gotten to court too early.

When a verdict is about to be announced, I like to arrive late, just before the judge takes his spot behind the bench. Every minute sitting at the defense table feels like a minute on the treadmill, which is to say it is endless.

But this time I've arrived well in advance, and I just sit and watch as the gallery fills up. Laurie is here, and Sam Willis, and Willie Miller.

Julie Traynor comes in, and before she takes her seat, she comes over and squeezes my arm. "Thank you."

Hike comes in, sits down, and shakes his head from side to side. "Too soon. Way too soon."

Jenna comes in with her team. We make eye contact and both get up and walk toward each other. We shake hands and she says, "I've enjoyed the battle."

"I wish I could say the same. I think I'm getting too old and cranky for this."

"I thought you were going to have your client testify."

I don't answer her; I just nod and we go back to our respective corners. She didn't mean it in a negative way, but the comment cuts right through me. If we lose, I'm going to attribute it to that decision, and it's going to be hard to deal with.

Finally the court clerk arrives and Noah is brought in, sure signs that we're about to start. "Do you have a prediction?" Noah asks me, the strain evident on his face and in his voice.

"Never. We wait and hope."

He nods. "I've been doing a lot of both."

Judge Stiller finally comes in; I feel like I've been sitting here since August. He puts the sternest look on his face that he can muster and warns the gallery not to react when the verdict is announced.

It's an empty warning. They will react, and he'll slam his gavel, and nobody will care. His power over them will be gone. The verdict boat will already have sailed.

He calls the jury in and asks the foreman if they have reached a verdict. He says that they have. I scan the faces of every one, trying to memorize them, because if they convict Noah, I am going to send Marcus after every last one of them.

Judge Stiller asks for the verdict to be brought to him. Everything is happening in slow motion; it always does in these situations. The judge reads the verdict to himself. It's an obnoxious process; there is no reason he can't wait like everyone else.

He betrays no emotion and keeps his face impassive, but inside he must feel like he's hot shit to be the only one besides the jury to know how this is going to end.

Judge Stiller tells the defendant to stand; for all I knew I was already standing. I get up along with Noah and Hike; I can't even feel my legs.

This never gets any easier.

The judge gives the verdict form back to the court clerk to read. A requirement for the position of court clerk must be that the applicant has to have the dullest voice imaginable. After three words of her monotone, everybody would be asleep if she wasn't revealing the fate of someone's life.

I always have to force my mind to concentrate in these situations. One would think I'd be completely focused, but it doesn't work that way, not for me. It's like my brain wants to escape to some other less stressful place. So I force myself to listen for the word *guilty* and focus on whether the word *not* is positioned in front of it.

"We the jury, in the case of the *State of New Jersey versus Noah Traynor,* find the defendant, Noah Traynor, not guilty of the crime of murder in the first degree."

I'm pretty sure I've heard it correctly, and that is confirmed when Noah hugs me. I look into the gallery and see the smile on Laurie's face as she hugs Julie Traynor, who is sobbing into her shoulder.

Life, at least for the moment, is once again good.

This is not the typical post-trial victory party.

We're doing it on Saturday afternoon, and rather than taking over Charlie's, we're located in an upstairs large private room there. The owners of Charlie's have made this accommodation because they are friends of mine and because on behalf of Vince, Pete, and myself, I have purchased about half a million beers over the years. And maybe two hundred thousand burgers.

The afternoon time and the special room are because of the unusual guest list. It includes Ricky and Danny Traynor, who would have trouble staying up if we had the gathering at night. But also present are Tara, Sebastian, Murphy, and Simon. While dogs are not allowed in New Jersey restaurants, Pete Stanton's presence has provided a tacit Police Department blessing.

Vince is here as well. To enjoy free food

and beer, Vince and Pete would if necessary climb to the Mount Everest base camp at four o'clock in the morning. But in this case all they had to do was climb the steps to the second floor in midafternoon. They were pleasantly surprised to see that I had televisions brought into the room so we could all watch the Giants lose a playoff game.

The other celebrating humans, besides Laurie and me, are Julie and Noah Traynor, Sam, Hike, Willie, Sondra, Edna, Marcus, and Corey Douglas.

Victory parties are always upbeat because they involve, well . . . victory. In this case it's sort of extra-special because it reunites Noah with his wife and son. Danny hasn't stopped smiling since we got here.

"Looks like your record as the Christmas-wish genie is intact," I say to Laurie.

"Admit it," she says. "It feels good."

"I admit it."

Noah and Julie walk over to thank Laurie and me; if they thank us one more time, it will officially break the all-time indoor thank-you record.

"Time for me to get back to work," Noah says. "I wrote a lot in jail, but it isn't exactly upbeat stuff." He smiles. "I wonder why."

"There was a lot of media and public attention paid to this case and trial," I say.

"Maybe a book might be a good idea?"

He nods. "I've already started to plan it. If I get an advance, I can starting paying your fee."

"Read my lips," Laurie says. "There is no fee. Seeing Danny and his father together is all the fee Andy wants."

Laurie has clearly never been to law school; she has a fundamental misunderstanding of the economics of the profession. I'm going to need to draw a line on this right here and now, but unfortunately I forgot to bring my crayons. So instead I just smile and nod.

Corey Douglas comes over, with Simon at his side. That dog is completely devoted to him. "Here are the reasons I am still alive and able to continue not collecting fees," I say.

Instead of acknowledging his saving my life in the park, Corey says to Laurie, "Did you tell him?"

"No. I was about to."

"Tell me what?" I ask.

Laurie, instead of answering, calls over to Marcus to join us, which he does. Then she turns back to me. "You seem to have a tendency to avoid taking on new cases."

"I try."

"But if you don't have clients, then we as

investigators have nothing to investigate. Which means we have no work."

"So you're thanking me for giving you extended vacations?"

"I think I should probably just come out and say it. Corey, Marcus, and I . . . along with Simon, of course . . . we are going into business together. We are starting an investigation firm, and we even have a name. We're calling it the K Team, because of Simon."

"*Canine* starts with a *c*," I point out.

"I don't think you're seeing the big picture here. But if you are worried, don't be. When you take on cases, you will be our most important client. And if our work requires a lawyer, you will have first option."

"Yunhh," Marcus says, eliminating any confusion that might exist.

I'm not sure how I feel about this news. I'm sort of feeling left out, but I want to be left out.

"You guys will be a great team," I say, because they will be a great team. I raise my glass of Diet Coke. "To the K Team."

It doesn't turn out to be a great toast because I'm the only one holding a glass. But they get the idea.

A trial, at least for me, is about answering questions.

If I like the answers, I tell them to the jury. If I don't, I try to keep them to myself. But basically it is a search for truth, and that truth is reached by answering questions. And usually it works pretty well.

But I like to have all the questions answered, even if just for my own peace of mind. When it comes to that, the Noah Traynor trial didn't end satisfactorily at all.

When no open issues are left in my mind after a trial, I would never consider looking at the trial documents again. Instead I would always pack them up and give them to Edna to file, and within a couple of years she'd get around to doing it.

In this case more issues are open than closed. I have tried to answer some questions from the very beginning and have just been unable to. Fortunately, the big one has been resolved. Arthur Wainwright is responsible for Karen McNeil's death.

I don't believe he did it himself; the actual killer no doubt was one of the unsavory characters who have themselves since bitten the dust. If I had to take a guess, my vote would be on Taillon, but that doesn't matter now. Arthur willed it and Arthur paid for it.

But the key question, the one I've been asking myself since the day I took the case, is why? Why was Kristen McNeil killed?

Everything else follows from that. What was Kristen so afraid of that she was running away? How did Charles Arrant, international criminal on the run from Interpol, wind up on a killing spree in Paterson, New Jersey? Whatever Arrant was doing here, had he finished his mission, or is someone else here to take his place?

How did Arrant know that Mitch Holzer knew his name and told it to me, and why did that represent such a threat that he killed Holzer and tried to do the same to me? Arthur Wainwright killed himself before I unloaded the big guns in court . . . the phone calls he received from Taillon around the time of Kristen's death, and of course the letter that she left. How did Arthur know those revelations were coming?

The Wainwright suicide is particularly troubling for me, and not just because I feel some guilt for having precipitated it. This guy spent sixty-plus years growing a business, a fortune, and an impeccable reputation. He was smart and resourceful; why did he think he couldn't survive what I was throwing at him? Why did he give up so easily?

The questions go on and on. The answers? Not so much.

So once again I turn to the dreaded trial documents, both the discovery and all the stuff we generated internally. Looking at them now is not quite like looking at them before the verdict; that hovering dread of failure is not there.

It's sort of like taking an SAT after you've been admitted to college. I'm driven by a nostalgic curiosity, but there's nothing urgent about it.

Not surprisingly, I spend three hours learning absolutely nothing. It's unsettling to me in that Arrant and Wainwright seemed to know what we were doing, yet it's inconceivable that any member of our group did any leaking.

I discuss it with Laurie, and she says, "Let me get Roger Carrasco in here, just in case."

I know who she's talking about. Roger is a

former colleague of Laurie's in the Police Department who now works in private surveillance. We've used him before to come in and make sure our home and my office were not being bugged. He does a full sweep for listening devices, webcams, phone taps, et cetera. He also checks our computers and cell phones for any evidence of infiltration.

"You think we're being bugged?" I ask.

"I have no idea, but it would explain it. We talked about Holzer and Arrant in the house, and we certainly talked about the letter that Kristen McNeil wrote."

Laurie calls Roger, and he's at our house within an hour. Two hours go by before he determines that there are no signs of surveillance devices anywhere. He goes down to check out my office, but I'm sure the result will be the same. We haven't spent that much time there, and as an example, I was not in the office between the time the McNeils gave me the letter and Karen testified in court.

Sure enough, since the office is small, Roger goes through it in less than an hour and calls with his report.

The place is clean.

Back to the documents.

Two things about the letter that Kristen wrote bug me.

One is that it appeared too conveniently; after fourteen years it was discovered just before I needed it at trial. I don't often get that lucky, and I distrust it when I do. But I can't figure out how its appearance could in any way be sinister because the McNeils certainly had no interest in getting Noah off the hook.

The other thing that bothers me, though not as much, is that in the letter Kristen mentions that she had saved money, and that therefore her parents shouldn't worry about her. Noah had told me that Kristen said she needed him to take her away because she had no money, and Kristen's friend Gale Halpern said that Kristen spent money faster than she made it. Gale even said that despite Kristen's earning a nice salary at NetLink, she was always borrowing from Gale.

This is not an earthshaking inconsistency. There are plenty of explanations. The most likely is that she was lying in the letter about having money so that her parents would worry less about her.

But it's worth checking out.

I call Karen McNeil and get her voice mail. I assume she is at work at the hospital, so I leave a message for her to call me back. She does, about an hour later.

"How are you doing?" I ask.

"Okay. Better than my parents, but they're getting through it, processing all that's happened. I think things will get better from here, now that we know who did it. We're all grateful to you for making sure the real truth came out."

"I want to ask you a question about Kristen's letter. She mentioned that she had saved plenty of money, but other people have told me that she never saved a dime in her life, that she spent it as fast as she made it. Did that strike you as strange?"

"I guess it did, but I just thought she was saying it to ease my parents' mind."

"I thought of that as well."

"But . . ." Karen stops.

I am looking forward to hearing the rest of this sentence. "But what?"

"There were a couple of things that were strange about that letter. Things were so emotional I hadn't focused on them, but I've thought about them since."

"Keep going."

"Well, for one thing, she called our parents 'Mother and Father.' Kristen just didn't talk like that; she wasn't nearly that formal. She called them 'Mom and Dad,' always."

"It was an unusual letter; maybe she felt the need to be more formal."

"I don't think so because of the other thing that bothers me. That was even stranger. She signed the letter 'Kris.'"

"So?"

"So Kristen hated the name Kris; she'd never let anyone call her that. She thought it made her sound like a boy."

"So you think she may not have written it?"

"No, she wrote it; I'm sure of that. I recognized her handwriting even before your expert confirmed it."

"You think she wrote it, but those aren't her words? And maybe she used 'Mother' and 'Father' and 'Kris' so you would realize that?"

Karen pauses for a few moments before answering. "I can't say that. She was under tremendous stress, right? Maybe it made her talk differently."

"Here's a tough one for you. Would she be smart enough to change those words deliberately, to tip you off that she was being forced to write it?"

Karen thinks for a few more moments. "Maybe. One thing people never seemed to understand about my sister. She was really smart."

I hope that I'm seeing things that aren't there.

I hope that the letter from Kristen was written just as originally represented, in advance of her expecting to leave on her own, probably with Noah. Because if that isn't how it happened, if she was forced to write it, then nothing is as it seemed.

It would mean that Arthur Wainwright, the man who killed himself because Andy Carpenter accused him of murder in open court, was innocent. Arthur, or a killer hired by Arthur, would not have forced Kristen to write a letter implicating Arthur in the murder. That would make no sense whatsoever.

But it physically can't have happened that way. The only way Kristen could have been forced to write that letter would be if she was under threat from her ultimate killer. But the letter was hidden in her desk drawer, waiting to be placed where her parents would find it, after she had run away.

If someone had forced Kristen to write it, someone who was set on implicating Arthur in the murder, they would have done a better job of it. They would have maneuvered a way to get the letter into the hands of her parents, not hidden in a place where it might not be discovered for fourteen years, if at all.

Besides, Arthur was wealthy, and Arrant, Taillon, and even Siroka were not in this for the thrill of the hunt. Whatever was going on, Arthur was in a unique position to finance it.

It has to be Arthur.

I am now in this all the way, which means I will bring Laurie back into it. She often sees things that I don't, but just talking it out is helpful and clears my mind. It's a very different situation from what I usually face in that I don't have a client to worry about and protect. I can just follow it where it goes, without worrying about the repercussions.

Laurie thinks it unlikely that Kristen was forced to write the letter. "She was obviously under incredible stress, even if she wrote it without coercion. The fact that she might have used a few names or words that were uncharacteristic seems understandable."

"You're probably right, but let's follow it through." It's a technique I always use when a status quo is questioned. I assume the new scenario is correct, just for the moment and just for the purpose of seeing where it leads.

Laurie nods. "The most obvious conclusion is that it would mean Arthur Wainwright was not involved in Kristen's murder. He wouldn't force her to write a letter accusing himself."

I nod. "No question."

"And if he didn't do it, there would have been very little reason for him to commit suicide, at least not that we know of. And especially since he was dead before you introduced testimony about Taillon's phone calls to him, and before Karen read the letter in court."

"It has to be him," I say. "Although something about the suicide bothers me."

"What's that?"

"The location."

"The cemetery?"

"Yes, but more because it was at his ex-wife's grave site. Kyle's college roommate told me that Kyle used to tell stories about their divorce, how bitter it was and how Arthur left her with almost nothing. Kyle hated him for it, which was why the roommate thought it was surprising and amusing that Kyle wound up working for him."

"Maybe it was a love-hate thing, and as he was about to die, love came back in the picture."

"Maybe."

"You think it wasn't a suicide?"

"If he didn't kill Kristen, which is the hypothetical we're currently working on, then I think it's very possible he was killed and it was set up to look like a suicide. If you wanted to do it in a place where you wouldn't be seen —"

She interrupts and finishes the thought. "What could work better than a secluded area of a cemetery, in the middle of the night, with a snowstorm about to start?"

"Right. And there is something else that I just thought of. It's the timing."

"What about the timing?"

"It's always been a little surprising that Arthur did what he did before the most damning evidence came out. I've assumed he somehow knew what was about to happen and bailed out rather than face it. But I never got the sense that Arthur was the type to back down; he was a fighter. He already hired a top lawyer in Hauser to go after me."

"So?"

"So maybe whoever was behind this knew what was going on and knew Arthur was about to come at me with both barrels. So he did what he had to do to stop him."

"How would the killer have known what was going to happen? We've already checked the place for bugs, so that couldn't be it."

"Beats the hell out of me. Sounds like a job for the K Team."

"Are you upset by Marcus, Corey, and me doing this, Andy?"

"No, of course not. But if you happen to be working on one of my cases, should I ever get stuck on another case, can you call it the A Team?"

"First of all, I think that name is taken. Second of all, when you act like this, we might have a different view of what *A* stands for."

I've spent another two hours this morning getting nowhere.

Our theories about Karen's letter and Arthur's involvement are interesting and maybe even credible, but we have no way to confirm or refute them. Which in term renders them useless.

"I'm going for a ride," I say to Laurie.

"Where to?"

"I need to drop the rent check off at Sofia's." I'm talking about the fruit stand below my office, owned and operated by Sofia Hernandez.

"Are you familiar with the concept of mail?"

"I am. But you know that when I drop it off, she gives me a cantaloupe. I live for her cantaloupes. Our mailman doesn't give me anything."

I get in the car and head down to my office. I'm still thinking about Arthur Wainwright, and I almost get into an accident because I should be thinking about driving. The driver of the car I almost rear-ended gives me the finger and drives away. I refrain from returning the gesture because I'm mature, and because the guy is right.

I park right in front of the office, which means right in front of Sofia Hernandez's fruit stand. She's behind the counter, casting a wary eye on the two teenage boys picking out fruit; my guess is there are a significant number of apple thefts that cut into her profit margin.

She lights up when she sees me. "Mr. Andy, how are you today?"

I have no idea why she puts *Mr.* in front of my name; I have tried to get her to stop on many occasions, obviously without success. "Very good, Sofia. How are you?"

"I'm good, family is good, but the fruit business is slow. I'm ready for summer."

We talk some more and I mention that I've come down to pay the rent. "You're always on time. You and Mr. Sam." She's referring to her other prize tenant, Sam Willis.

I hand her the envelope with the check.

"I forgot to tell you. I have PayPal now, you don't have to give me the checks. You can pay that way."

"That's okay; I don't mind. I like seeing you." The truth is that I wouldn't know how to use PayPal if you gave me a year to figure it out.

"You just want your cantaloupe." She smiles.

I return the smile. "You know me too well."

She gives me the cantaloupe. I have no idea how she gets ripe ones year-round, but I'm not complaining. We thank each other and I head back home, cherished cantaloupe on the seat next to me, setting off the alarm because I haven't fastened the cantaloupe's seat belt.

I'm on the way home, stopped at a light on Market Street, near Eastside High School. I'm smiling to myself over Sofia Hernandez using PayPal and, unlike me, trying to avoid becoming a technological dinosaur.

Then I wonder how many of my law school colleagues are paying rent to landlords who run fruit stands.

Then I say to myself, out loud, "Holy shit."

The first thing I do when I get home, even before I update Laurie on what is going on, is call Sam Willis. "Sam, I've got some things I want you to do."

"We have a new client?"

"No. Same one."

"Oh." I can hear the disappointment in his voice. "What do you need?"

"Send me information on routers . . . how they work, general stuff. You can email it to me at the office."

"Routers? How technical do you want me to get?"

"Doesn't matter; I'm not going to read it. Also include whatever information about Kyle Wainwright you can find online. Doesn't matter what it is; I'm not going to read that either. Then I want you to talk to Sofia Hernandez and . . . hey, do you think you can hack into the computers of a university?"

"Why? You want me to change your grades?"

"Sam . . ."

"Of course I can get in. Those eggheads think they're so smart they never protect themselves well enough."

"Great." I tell him what the situation is and what I want him to do.

"I'm on it." The disappointment is gone from his voice.

As soon as I get off the phone with Sam, I call Pete Stanton. He gets on with "I don't like those midafternoon victory parties. By eight o'clock I was hungry again."

"Maybe if you'd stop arresting the wrong people, I wouldn't win so many cases, and we wouldn't need to have parties."

"Maybe I should arrest you for impersonating an asshole. What are you calling me for?"

"I know what's going on."

"Going on with what?"

"Kristen McNeil, Arthur Wainwright, Charles Arrant, everything."

I'm sure he can tell by my voice that I'm serious. "I'm listening."

"You're going to have to do more than that. I'm just not ready quite yet. And you're not going to like it, but you're going to have to play by my rules."

Kyle Wainwright figured he had mourned long enough.

There was a business to run. NetLink Systems was now his business; his father's will was clearly written to leave it to him. There were other co-owners, but Arthur had 65 percent, which gave him full control. Which meant that Kyle was now in full control.

Kyle pretended to the outside world that he was upset about his father's death, but he didn't bother pretending it to himself. He could not stand the son of a bitch, ever since he'd bailed out on Kyle and his mother. But Kyle kept his eye on the financial ball, and now it had paid off.

Kyle was a smart guy, and he had carefully watched how his father ran things. Kyle had also watched Jeremy Kennon and the other tech guys and had learned from them. Kyle felt confident that he knew the business inside and out, and that he was ready.

But NetLink Systems was not quite the company it was a few days ago. The circumstances of Arthur's death carried with them a lot more than the whiff of scandal. NetLink's clients were going to be worried that they would be tainted by association, and they would need to be treated with kid gloves.

Countering that was that NetLink was an outstanding company that turned out an excellent product, and they had contracts in place with all of their important clients. By the time those contracts neared their end, the scandal would have faded, and things should continue as always.

Kyle would devote himself to making the clients comfortable; he was good at that. He would do whatever was necessary to ensure success.

He had waited too long. Nothing was going to stop him.

Jeremy Kennon is not there when I call, so I leave a message.

I've created a rather significant upheaval at NetLink Systems, to say the least, so I'm not sure if he'll call me back. But he's been willing to talk in the past, so I'm hoping he will.

He does . . . fifteen minutes later. "Haven't you caused enough damage already? What the hell do you want now?"

"To talk."

"So talk." His tone of voice makes it clear that we're not necessarily buddies anymore.

"It has to be in person; I don't want to do it over the phone. And I have some theories to share with you that I need your input on. You have the expertise."

"You want my input? What am I, on your staff? Tell me what this is about."

"Arthur and Kyle Wainwright. Not necessarily in that order."

"What about them?"

"Can we meet? There is something you need to hear, and some things for you to explain to me. You're the only one who can do it."

He thinks for a few moments. "You sure as hell can't come here to the office, not after what happened with Arthur."

"You pick the place."

"How about my house? I live in Ridgewood."

"No good. The place could be bugged. Surveillance is what we're going to be talking about."

"Come on, bugged? Who are you, James Bond?" Then, "So you pick the place."

"The Duck Pond in Ridgewood. Should be convenient for you."

"The Duck Pond? This is January."

"Dress warm . . . believe me, this is important. Eight o'clock? Near where the picnic tables are?"

"I should not be doing this. Eight o'clock."

I get off the phone and check my emails for the information on routers and Kyle Wainwright that Sam sent me. I just skim it briefly, but everything seems to be in order. Then I call him to get the updates on the other areas he was checking into, and everything he says fits neatly into place.

Then I talk to Laurie about the arrangements I think we should make, all of which she agrees with.

And then all I can do is wait to meet with Jeremy Kennon. If all goes well, that will click the last piece neatly into place.

I arrive at the Duck Pond at ten before eight.

It's dark and cold here, not terribly unexpected for a northern New Jersey night in early January. I'm also not crazy about being in a dark place, all alone, but I have no reason to think I won't be safe. And I also have no one to blame; I picked the time and place.

Kennon pulls up right on time and parks near me. He walks over, arms folded, slapping his sides to deal with the temperature. "This is nuts."

"I'll be as quick as I can. We can sit over there."

We sit at one of the picnic tables, across from each other. "Okay, let's hear it."

"Arthur Wainwright had been running an illegal operation out of NetLink Systems. He started it soon after he founded the company, and it's been ongoing ever since.

He did it alone; there was no need to include anyone else. Ultimately, he brought in Kyle."

"What kind of illegal operation?" I've obviously got Kennon's attention.

"It has to do with the routers. There's a chip in there . . . at least I guess it's a chip. This really isn't my area; that's what I need you for. But when a router with that chip was placed in a company, or even in a private person's home, it allowed Arthur to monitor everything that came in on the internet into that network."

Kennon doesn't respond, so I continue, "So in effect they were spying on companies all over the country; maybe the world. They got the most intimate details of a company's operations, strategies, plans. You know how much that information would be worth to certain people? I'm sure you do.

"That's where Arrant came in. He was the conduit for all of it. He was international, so my guess is that there is spying involving a number of countries as well. There is no limit to what they might pay for industrial espionage with that kind of value. But that isn't for me to go through; that will be up to the authorities once we break this open."

"We?"

I nod. "You're the key player. You know

the ins and outs of your systems. You can figure out how all this was done. This is the right time to get on the right side of this, Jeremy."

"What if you're wrong?"

"Fair enough. I'll give you an example. One of the routers NetLink made is used in the athletic department at Clemson University. A coach at LSU, going through Arrant, paid for their offensive game plan. I'm not sure if you saw the game, but LSU won, twenty-one to six."

"Arthur has been out of the tech area for a while."

I nod. "But Kyle hasn't. Kyle has been dealing with Arrant directly. The beauty of it is that no one else at NetLink had to know about it. All Kyle had to do was insert the chip, and no one could ever know that it was bad."

"Is that it?"

I nod. "Yes, except for one other thing. There's just one mistake in all I've told you so far."

"What's that?"

"Instead of using the name Kyle Wainwright, I should have used Jeremy Kennon."

The expression on his face is surprise, not worry. "What the hell does that mean?"

"It means you've been conducting the

operation, with Arrant. It means you killed Arthur Wainwright. It means that you were the older man Kristen McNeil was having an affair with. And it means you hired Taillon to kill Kristen McNeil, after he forced her to write the letter.

"Taillon didn't call Arthur's private line back then. He was calling you. You told me that the company was always changing offices, moving people around. I'm betting they didn't redo the whole phone system each time, so the private numbers stayed with the office."

Kennon lets this all sink in, then says, in a quieter, calmer voice than I would expect, "How did you figure it out?"

"It started with something you said. When you were at my office, you asked if I pick up a cantaloupe when I drop off my rent check. I didn't think anything of it, but looking back, I wondered how you possibly could have assumed that the person who ran the fruit stand was my landlord.

"So we talked to her. We asked her about the day last month when we lost wireless internet, and she said someone from the computer company had come by and installed newer equipment that day, without her even asking for it. And guess what? The new router was made by NetLink Systems.

"You were reading every email I got. That's how you knew about Mitch Holzer mentioning Arrant's name to me. And you read my email to my lawyer colleague about finding Kristen's letter. That's why you jumped the gun and killed Arthur; you didn't want him defending himself. No telling what might have come out."

"Not bad," Kennon said. "But if you were looking to break this open, why are you telling me? Why not the police?"

"Did I mention the money that you must be making? I want some of it, and I want some for my client. Payment for the nightmare you put him through."

Kennon stands up; and somehow a gun has appeared in his hand. "I don't think so. You made a big mistake; you've set the whole thing up for Kyle to take the fall. It will look like he did all of this, including killing you." Kennon looks around. "You even picked a great location. Maybe better than the cemetery. Let's take a walk towards those trees."

Suddenly there is a sound I have now gotten familiar with, followed by a blur that runs across my line of vision and lands on Kennon. He screams and within an instant he is on the ground, Simon ripping at his arm.

"Off," Corey says, and the ever-obedient Simon obeys. Freed from the crazy dog, Kennon tries to run, only to be grabbed by Marcus and tossed like a tennis ball against a tree. He falls to the ground.

"Nicely done, boys," says Laurie.

Suddenly the area is lit up by floodlights; it's now daytime at the Duck Pond. Pete runs up, flanked by three officers with guns drawn.

I open my shirt, which does not feel good in the cold, and I rip the wire off my chest, which feels even worse. "You get it all?"

Pete nods. "Every word."

"Pete," I say, "have you met the K Team?"

I can't sleep, so Laurie and I stay up late talking.

It's going to be August by the time the adrenaline wears off.

So we sit in the kitchen and try to figure out the parts of the conspiracy that we're not sure of. If Jeremy ever pleads guilty, maybe we'll have the last details confirmed.

"I think Kennon wanted to blame Arthur for Kristen's murder all along," I say. "That's why he forced her to write the letter. She wrote it just before he killed her."

"How did they get it in the house?"

"Karen had told me that there was a break-in at the house while everyone was at the funeral. Jewelry was taken, but I think that was a cover. They were just planting the letter."

"But they never followed up to find another way to implicate Arthur. When the letter wasn't found, they let him off the hook."

"Right. Because of the skin under her fingernails. The police were set on the person with that DNA being the killer. So Kennon had to back off, especially when Kristen's parents didn't find the letter. It worked out for him because Arthur backed out of the tech area, giving Kennon free rein."

"So now what?"

"Now the government will have to track down all these routers and figure out what's going on. Sam says it will be an impossible task, but that's not our problem. My next step will be to do a public interview, letting everyone know that Arthur Wainwright was neither a murderer nor a suicide victim. It's the very least I can do."

"Poor Noah," Laurie says. "Talk about being in the wrong place at the wrong time."

"But it all worked out because of your three-month Christmas season. If you hadn't gotten Danny's wish list when you did, Noah would be heading to prison for the rest of his life."

We head up to bed. Ricky is sleeping at Will Rubenstein's, so Laurie puts on some romantic music.

"Jingle Bells."

ABOUT THE AUTHOR

David Rosenfelt is the Edgar-nominated and Shamus Award-winning author of eleven stand-alones and nineteen Andy Carpenter novels, including *Bark of Night*. After years of living in California, he and his wife moved to Maine with twenty-five of the four thousand dogs they have rescued.

The employees of Thorndike Press hope you have enjoyed this Large Print book. All our Thorndike, Wheeler, and Kennebec Large Print titles are designed for easy reading, and all our books are made to last. Other Thorndike Press Large Print books are available at your library, through selected bookstores, or directly from us.

For information about titles, please call:
(800) 223-1244

or visit our website at:
gale.com/thorndike

To share your comments, please write:
Publisher
Thorndike Press
10 Water St., Suite 310
Waterville, ME 04901